It couldn't be...

Santi.

Her mother had sent Santi.

He was standing in front of Elsa before she could unfreeze her shocked brain, straight white teeth flashing in a wide smile, bearlike hands lightly gripping her shoulders. He leaned down and placed his cheek against hers as if this was a planned meeting between two close friends and whispered, "Smile and look pleased to see me."

But her shock was too great. The cologne she'd caught in ghostly fragments over the years had already engulfed her senses. The skin on her cheek tingled from the soft brush of his beard. Elsa reared back. Her frozen mouth managed to form one word. It came out like an accusation.

"You."

He tightened the hold on her shoulders and increased the wattage of his smile. "Me. Now, as delightful as this reunion is, we need to get moving."

His gravelly voice dived straight into her stunned senses. The courtyard began to swim around her. Of all the people in the world she'd have wanted to escort her home, Santiago "Santi" Rodriguez would have been at the very bottom of the list.

Billion-Dollar Mediterranean Brides

Reunions sealed with a diamond ring!

Sisters Elsa and Marisa Lopez grew up loved and wanting for nothing. Until their family came under threat from dangerous criminals intent on exploiting the Lopezes' lucrative shipping company. Their lives have already changed forever, but there's one more change they had better get ready for...when they reencounter the billionaires they've never been able to forget!

Elsa finds herself under the protection of the man she was infatuated with as a teenager, self-made tycoon Santi Rodriguez, in:

The Forbidden Innocent's Bodyguard

And look out for single mother Marisa's story, coming soon!

Michelle Smart

THE FORBIDDEN INNOCENT'S BODYGUARD

Recycling programs
for this product may
not exist in your area.

ISBN-13: 978-1-335-40410-7

The Forbidden Innocent's Bodyguard

Copyright © 2021 by Michelle Smart

This edition published by arrangement with Harlequin Books S.A.

For questions and comments about the quality of this book,
please contact us at CustomerService@Harlequin.com.

Harlequin Enterprises ULC
22 Adelaide St. West, 40th Floor
Toronto, Ontario M5H 4E3, Canada
www.Harlequin.com

Printed in U.S.A.

Michelle Smart's love affair with books started when she was a baby, when she would cuddle them in her cot. A voracious reader of all genres, she found her love of romance established when she stumbled across her first Harlequin book at the age of twelve. She's been reading—and writing—them ever since. Michelle lives in Northamptonshire, England, with her husband and two young smarties.

Books by Michelle Smart

Harlequin Presents

Her Sicilian Baby Revelation

Cinderella Seductions

A Cinderella to Secure His Heir
The Greek's Pregnant Cinderella

Passion in Paradise

A Passionate Reunion in Fiji
His Greek Wedding Night Debt

The Delgado Inheritance

The Billionaire's Cinderella Contract
The Cost of Claiming His Heir

The Sicilian Marriage Pact

A Baby to Bind His Innocent

Visit the Author Profile page
at Harlequin.com for more titles.

To Millie, happy reading x

CHAPTER ONE

ELSA LOPEZ COULDN'T stop pacing. She'd spent the past week hiding in her Viennese apartment obeying her mother's request to stay inside until the man tasked with escorting her home to Valencia arrived, and her nerves were shredded.

Her usually unobtrusive security detail had quadrupled with no warning a week ago. She now had a bodyguard stationed outside her front door, another guarding the front entrance to the apartment building and another guarding the back entrance. In a top-floor apartment on the other side of the courtyard were more guards watching every person who came within its vicinity. Her trip home to Valencia for her sister's engagement party had been bought forward. Her mother wanted her home and within the safety of the Lopez estate as soon as possible. That could only mean there had been a specific threat against Elsa.

Still pacing, she read her mother's latest cryptic email again. Their communications were supposed to be secure but both women worked on the assumption that every call was listened to and every written communication read. After what had happened to their family, paranoia was to be expected. Jumping at shadows had become a part of Elsa's life.

Be ready to leave on the day of Samson's birth. Your escort has made all the arrangements. Trust him. Trust no one else.

Samson had been Elsa and her sister Marisa's first pet. Their parents had bought the dog for them when they'd been in infant school. They'd faithfully celebrated his birthday on the ninth of July for every one of his twelve years of life.

Today was the ninth of July.

There was a rap on her front door. She checked the security camera before opening it, just in case. Since her father's murder a year ago, 'Just in case' had become something of a mantra.

'Your escort has arrived,' the unsmiling guard told her.

'Is he one of your men?'

He shook his head.

'Who is he?'

Her question went unanswered. The guard indicated the oversized handbag sitting by the door. 'Is this all you're taking?'

She picked it up and secured it over her shoulder. 'Yes.' She always travelled light when she returned to Valencia. She'd lived in Vienna for five years, but her childhood bedroom was still hers, the wardrobes still stuffed with all her clothes and accessories. All she'd packed were her cosmetics, purse and passport.

Elsa's apartment was set above a pizzeria and book shop in a beautiful building with white walls and green window frames. She followed the guard down the narrow stairs to the ground floor and stepped out into the cobbled courtyard. Mid-morning and the coffee shop on the other side was spilling over with people. Summer in Vienna was hitting its stride, the students and hipsters who usually made up the bodies wandering through this laid-back district increasing rather than decreasing in numbers.

A tall, well-built figure with a full, thick black beard standing propped against a lamppost caught her attention. Arms with biceps the size of her thighs were folded across a powerfully built chest. There was something familiar about him, something that made her heart give a sudden jolt. Shielding her eyes against the glare of the rising sun, she stopped walking and stared.

It couldn't be…?

She dropped her hand from her brow and stared some more. The figure moved towards her. Incongruously dressed for the weather and bohemian vibe of the district in a pair of dark grey trousers, a dark blue shirt unbuttoned at the neck and a charcoal waistcoat, the unruly curly black hair had been slicked back, dark shades along with the new beard covering much of the face she'd tried her hardest to forget.

Santi.

Her mother had sent Santi.

He was standing in front of her before she could unfreeze her shocked brain, straight white teeth flashing in a wide smile, bear-like hands lightly gripping her shoulders. He leaned down and placed his cheek against hers as if this was a planned meeting between two close friends and whispered, 'Smile and look pleased to see me.'

But her shock was too great. The cologne she'd caught in ghostly fragments over the years had already engulfed her senses. The skin on her cheek tingled from the soft brush of his beard. Elsa reared back. Her frozen mouth managed to form one word. It came out like an accusation.

'You.'

He tightened the hold on her shoulders and increased the wattage of his smile. 'Me. Now, as delightful as this reunion is, we need to get moving.'

His gravelly voice dived straight into her stunned senses. The courtyard began to swim around her. Of all the people in the world she'd have wanted to escort her home, Santiago 'Santi' Rodriguez would have been at the very bottom of the list.

It had been five years since Elsa had left his bed crushed, shamed and chastened but those years melted away and, cheeks now burning under the weight of his stare, the old humiliation slapped her afresh.

In desperation, she turned to the bodyguard who'd accompanied her but he'd melted away too.

Santi hid his impatience and kept the smile on his face as he released Elsa's slender shoulders to take her hand. She tried to jerk away but he didn't relinquish his hold. 'We don't have time for this, *chiquita*. We need to move. Now smile and come with me.'

Tugging at her hand, he set off, forcing her to move alongside him.

'Of all the places you could have set up home, you had to choose a pedestrianised area?' he joked in an effort to ease the tension as they weaved through the crowds and onto Mariahilfer Strasse. 'I thought I might have to kill someone for a parking space.'

She didn't respond. Her pretty face was clenched from smooth brow to heart-shaped chin.

Using his excellent internal sense of direction—Santi had never been lost in his life, had only to look at a map once to memorise it—they crossed the wide road bursting with shoppers and slipped down a side street. Although Elsa trotted beside him in mute obedience, he didn't release her hand. His intuition, which was as excellent as his sense of direction, told him strongly that should he let her go, she would bolt.

After the way she'd ignored him at her father's funeral, he hadn't expected her to greet him with whoops of joy but did she have to act so repulsed when he was putting his life on the line for her? The woman who'd once been his little shadow now recoiled from him. The first word she'd spoken to him in five years had been hissed at him as if he were dirt on his shoe.

The last time they'd spoken was the night he'd found her in his bed. Considering how drunk she'd been, he'd be surprised if she remembered any of it, actions *or* words.

He'd done his damned best to forget it too.

They reached the Naschmarkt, a mile-long market already bursting at the seams with locals and tourists. If anyone was following them, this was where Santi intended to shake them off. Keeping a firm hold of Elsa's hand, he cut through food stalls and restaurants, backtracked a few times, cut through a coffee bar and then led her outside and down another side street where the car he'd acquired was parked.

Elsa took one look at the tiny, battered white car and raised a brow. 'You're saving me from what I assume are kidnappers in *that*?' The car had to be the same age as her and could in no way be called a classic.

He grinned and unlocked the passenger door manually. 'If you aren't expecting it then the kidnappers aren't either.'

This confirmation of her suspicions hit her like a needle of ice being injected directly into her veins and she grabbed hold of the opened door to stop her weakening legs dropping her to the ground.

Santi must have read something on her face for his smile fell. 'You didn't know?'

She tried to get moisture into her arid mouth. 'I knew there was a threat to me but not the details,' she croaked. 'Mamá said my escort…you, I suppose…would explain.'

'I'll explain everything once we're on the road,' he promised.

In the car, she dropped her head between her knees

and breathed deeply. At least she hadn't fainted. That was one good thing.

Santi leaned in through the driver's door. 'I need your phone.'

'Why?' she asked dimly.

'They're probably tracking it.'

Mutely, head still dipped, she pulled it out of her bag and handed it to him. He dropped it to the ground. It crunched beneath his giant foot.

'I have a replacement for you in the boot.'

'Okay,' she whispered.

'Are *you* okay?'

She raised her head and took another deep breath. 'I'm fine.'

'Then buckle up, *chiquita*, and let's get this heap of junk to the airport.'

Only when he'd turned the engine on did she cast him a sideways glance. The sick, faint feeling that had enveloped her disappeared and she was suddenly struck by an urge to laugh. All six feet four of pure muscle that was Santiago Rodriguez was folded into the driver's seat. His head skimmed the roof, his knees touching the steering wheel so intimately he could use them to drive.

He flashed the grin that had once made her insides melt and put the heap of junk into gear. With a screech of tyres, they were off.

Elsa stared out of the window while they drove out of the city she'd made her home. Her heart had lodged in her throat. When would she next see her apartment? Sit at her desk in the calm open-plan office? Enjoy a quiet cappuccino with a good book at her favourite coffee shop? Would she ever feel safe again? Would she ever *be* safe again?

When they were safely crawling on the Ost Autobahn, she cleared her throat. 'You said you were going to tell me everything.'

Santi waited until the articulated lorry overtaking them had safely passed before answering. 'How much do you know about the efforts to bring the cartel who killed your father to justice?'

The dizzy, nauseous feeling started up again, white noise buzzing in her ears at the mention of the cartel.

Elsa's family owned a shipping company that transported freight across the world. Fifteen months ago, a representative of the cartel in question approached her parents offering a ridiculous amount of money to use their cargo ships to smuggle drugs. Her parents said no. The cartel increased their monetary offer. Her parents still said no. The next day they found their dog, Buddy, drowned in the swimming pool. Things escalated from there. Her parents refused to be intimidated and called the police. They also increased their personal security.

Three months after the cartel's initial approach, Elsa's father Marco had kissed her mother goodbye and set off for a round of golf. While he'd played eighteen holes with his regular golfing friends, someone had tampered with the brakes of his car. Whether they'd intended for him to die or just wanted to scare him was irrelevant. Marco Lopez had driven into the back of a delivery truck at a set of traffic lights five hundred yards from the golf course and died instantly.

'I know the new security guy Mamá hired, that Felipe Lorenzi, has a team working to bring them down,' Elsa croaked.

'Things have moved quickly in the last month. International authorities are involved. They've been putting the final pieces into place to make a co-ordinated swoop on the cartel and arrest them. One of Felipe's men received a tip-off that the cartel have got wind of it and are planning pre-emptive action.'

She could hardly unfreeze her throat enough to whisper, 'Me?'

'Yes. They want to frighten your mother into dropping her evidence. Right now it's the only solid non-circumstantial evidence the authorities have against them.'

A day after her husband's death, Rosaria Lopez had received a phone call from the cartel's representative. The caller had commiserated about Marco's death then casually asked about the health of her heavily pregnant daughter Marisa. The threat had been implicit. Rosaria had agreed to a meeting with the representative, which she'd attended wearing a pair of teardrop earrings with a recording device implanted in them. Elsa still struggled to comprehend how her formidable but grieving mother had found the courage to walk into the lion's den, but walk into it she had and, during the conversation in which the cartel had laid out their fresh demands, came a concrete admission of guilt for Marco's death. And more threats.

The cartel were satisfied they had the Lopezes in their pocket. They completely underestimated the Lopez women's steel. Rosaria made numerous copies of the recording, fired her security team and, on Santi's advice, hired Felipe Lorenzi in their place. Felipe's team beefed up their protection and formed an impenetrable fortress around them. Communications from the cartel suddenly ceased. None of the Lopez women dared believe that would be the last they heard from them, and set about bringing the cartel down before they could go for their family again.

Elsa tried to process this specific threat to her but there were so many emotions ravaging her that it was hard to get her thoughts in order. 'Why am I in your care and not Felipe's?'

'Your mother asked me,' he answered with a shrug. Santi couldn't be completely certain but he thought they'd escaped the city without being followed.

He thought back to the conversation of five days ago. He'd been sat in the garden with Rosaria and her elder daughter Marisa. Santi had been regularly updated about the situation, had thrown his own time and resources at assisting the Lopezes' fight for justice, and he'd listened to the revelation about the new specific threat to Elsa without a flicker of emotion.

Rosario had fixed the green-brown eyes her younger daughter had inherited on him. 'Bring her home to me, Santi,' she'd said.

Although he'd had a good idea she was going to ask him to do this and had learned skills over the past year in anticipation of something like this happening, he'd still sucked in a breath. 'Wouldn't it be better for Felipe and his men to bring her back? They're the experts.'

'They will give you every assistance but I trust *you*.' Tears had glistened in her eyes and her voice had caught before she could continue.

Marisa had been the one to finish for her. 'To them, Elsa's just another job.'

He'd understood. God help him, he'd understood.

Santi had been as near as dammit a part of the Lopez family since they'd employed his mother as their housekeeper when he'd been a boy of ten and Elsa had been incubating in Rosaria's womb. Everything he had and everything he was was because of this family. There was nothing he wouldn't do for them.

Elsa rested her head against the window and closed her eyes. Her parents had always believed the sun shone out of Santi's backside. She'd once believed that too.

A memory flashed in her mind. Her first house party without adult supervision. She'd been, what, fifteen? Sixteen? Her parents had, of course, believed there would be responsible adults there. It had never occurred to them that their baby girl would lie. She'd had a cigarette. It had made her cough so hard and had tasted so disgusting that she'd never touched another. One of her friends had smoked dope but Elsa's throat had been too sore from the coughing fit to try it for herself. She'd drunk beer, though. She hadn't liked the taste but there had been no other alcohol available, not that she'd found anyway.

As was often the case with unsupervised teenage house parties, alcohol and illicit drugs meant things got pretty raucous. When a game of Beer Pong resulted in a flat-screen television being smashed, Elsa had still been sober enough to know it was time to leave, and had sent a message to her dad asking to be collected.

A little woozy but still the right side of drunk, she'd waited out front with her friends Lola and Carmen. A handful of older boys joined them, boys the three virginal girls had whisperingly agreed were *sexy*. When offered a bottle of beer each, the giggling girls had accepted, too naïve to realise the boys expected payment.

That payment had been of the tongues down throats and hands up tops and down skirts variety. Elsa had never expected her first kiss to be of the drunken, unwanted kind, but that's what it had been. The boy in question hadn't even *asked*. It had been disgusting, all slobbery, like what she'd imagine kissing Rocco, her dad's English mastiff, would be like. She'd pushed him away. He'd grabbed hold of her again and pinned her hands behind her back to stop her resisting.

There hadn't been time for her to feel scared because that had been the moment a shadow had fallen over them and then suddenly the boy had released her and levitated… But he hadn't been levitating, she'd realised a blink later. He was hovering inches off the ground because Santi had hoiked him into the air by his neck.

He'd grinned at Elsa and, still holding the boy aloft with one hand, had dug into his pocket with the other and thrown his keys to her. 'Wait in the car for me, *chiquita*. And your friends.'

From the safety of the car, the three girls had stared with their faces pressed to the window as Santi entered the house. Moments later teenagers of differing stages of inebriation had flooded out.

When he'd finally joined the girls in the car, he'd told them to buckle up, turned the radio on and, singing along to the song playing, driven away.

'What did you do to that boy?' Elsa had asked after Santi dropped her friends at their homes. There had been no need to question why he'd collected her rather than her father. He'd always been happy to run errands for him and act as occasional chauffeur to the Lopez girls.

'Nothing you need worry about,' he'd answered.

'Did you hurt him?'

'How would you feel if I had?'

She'd thought about it. 'Good. But bad too.'

He'd laughed. 'I didn't hurt him or his scum friends, but I promise you this much—those boys are never going to manhandle you or any other female again.' His voice had then become serious. 'I want you to promise me that when you are out with your friends, you all look out for each other. I get that you're at an age where you want to experiment but you need to keep safe too and for women, safety comes in numbers. You understand?'

That was the night Elsa had fallen madly in love with Santiago Rodriguez. Overnight, the chiselled face with the broad nose, wide mouth and black eyes surrounded by lines that seemed permanently crinkled with amusement turned into the most handsome face she'd ever seen.

The next day she'd received an enormous bunch of flowers from the manhandling boy with a note that simply read, 'Sorry.' She'd received presents from Santi that day too—a rape alarm, a can of pepper spray and self-defence classes.

And now, as much as she wanted to seethe that her mother had entrusted her safety in the face of such danger to Santi, Elsa understood why she'd done so.

Santi would never let anything happen to her. He might have gained a fortune in his own right over the past decade that put her family's wealth to shame but he would put his own life on the line for any of the Lopezes. His loyalty was unwavering and eternal.

For all that being with him made her want to curl into a ball and cover her face, and for all that she hated him for his cold cruelty that night five years ago, the fear that had gnawed in her belly all week had settled. The old feeling of safety she'd always had when she'd been with him had smothered the fear.

Elsa was pulled from her trip down memory lane when Santi entered the car park of an airport hotel. He found a space near the entrance. She went to open her door but he put a hand on her arm.

'Wait.'

She waited.

When satisfied no suspicious cars had joined them,

he said, 'Follow my lead and save any questions until we're alone.'

Striding into the hotel, he headed straight to the reception. To her surprise, he produced two passports which he handed over with a credit card. A room key was given in return and then Elsa found herself being led to an elevator. Thinking he intended for them to stay hidden in a room until the last possible moment, she was further surprised when he pressed the button to the basement.

'Where are we going?'

The doors pinged open before he could answer, revealing a loading area for deliveries and rows of industrial bins, trolleys and other random items. The most random of all was a gleaming Aston Martin with tinted windows nestled between a row of overflowing green bins and a pile of discarded crates.

Santi waved an arm with a flourish. 'Your chariot awaits.'

'I know the other car was a hunk of junk but isn't this a bit excessive for a short drive to the airport terminal? Can't we take the shuttle?'

He raised his brow.

'What?'

'Didn't your *mamá* tell you? We're not flying to Valencia.'

'Then how are we getting home?'

White teeth slowly exposed themselves under his widening grin. 'We're taking the scenic route. You and I, *chiquita*, are going on a road trip.'

CHAPTER TWO

'A ROAD TRIP?' Elsa said dumbly. 'We're driving all the way to Valencia? But that will take...*days*.'

He pulled a musing face. 'There's some sailing involved too. But saying "road trip" has a much better ring to it than "road and sailing trip", don't you think? And speaking of which...' he opened the passenger door '...we need to get going. We only have a little breathing space. I want the airport to be dust before they realise they've lost you.'

She slid into the luxurious interior, put her bag between her feet and fastened her seat belt while Santi climbed into the driver's side. When he closed the door, the motion sent a waft of his cologne into her airwaves, a scent that was earthy and musky and made her breath catch in her throat and her abdomen clench.

'Can't we fly from a different airport?' she asked in desperation. 'Hire a small plane or, better still, take one of *your* planes. You know everything about the aviation industry. You can get us there undetected. We can be home by dinner.'

He sighed and pressed the start button. The engine

purred gently to life. 'Your family, Felipe and I agreed it would be better to take you home via the scenic route.'

'But driving and sailing?'

He put the car into Reverse and swung out of the parking space. 'The plan to bring down the cartel starts now, and we want you safe and far from the action while it happens. If the gods are smiling on us and Felipe and his men and the authorities do their jobs properly, the cartel will be history by the time we arrive in Valencia.' He nosed the car out of the hotel's delivery area, looked from right to left and pulled smoothly onto the road. 'It was all supposed to happen in a few weeks but the threat to you has bought it forward.'

'What about my family? Where have they been taken?'

'The villa's been turned into a fortress.'

Angry, terrified heat filled her head and she slammed her fists on her thighs. 'Why haven't they been *moved*?'

'Because that would have tipped the cartel off,' he answered calmly.

'And turning the villa into a fortress didn't do that?'

'The estate has been heavily guarded since your father's death. You know this. The extra security was brought in very discreetly.'

She threw him the filthiest glare she could muster before turning her face to the window and clamping her lips together.

Elsa didn't care how heavily guarded the estate was. She didn't care that the villa had a panic room with provisions that could keep her family protected and fed against a month-long siege. They should have been taken to a safe house in a different country. Somewhere like New Zealand.

'Your mother told you to trust me, *chiquita*,' he said, his gravelly voice suddenly soft. 'So trust me when I say your family are safe. Nothing will happen to them. I swear.'

Her throat was too choked to answer, eyes brimming with tears that were certain to unleash if she looked at him.

'Have I ever broken a promise to you before?' he asked gently.

Keeping her gaze out of the window, she gave a small shake of her head.

Promise not to tell my mamá.
Promise not to tell my papá.
Promise you'll get me there on time?
Promise you'll be there?
You promise?

Variations of promises she'd made him swear throughout her most formative teenage years. He'd kept every one of them. Got her out of more scrapes than she could remember.

And then he'd broken her heart.

Santi spent the next hour or so concentrating on the road before and behind them, watching for a tail. He didn't think anyone was following but wouldn't take anything for granted. Traffic was heavy but once they'd driven through Margarethen am Moos, it lightened and the tension in his shoulders loosened a little too.

While his remaining tension was all internal, Elsa was as taut as a wind-up clock. She needed to relax before rigor mortis set in. He had complete confidence in Felipe Lorenzi and his men. The Lopez family couldn't be safer if they were in Fort Knox.

He turned the radio on, found a station that played the kind of tunes he liked, and cranked the sound up. Santi had a special loathing for randomised non-curated playlists. In a world where technology and streaming ruled, he still preferred the human touch.

'How can you sing?' the rigid woman beside him asked accusingly.

'How can you not?' he retorted.

'Because...'

'Because you want to let your demons control you?'

When Santi felt the old familiar tension and anger stir in his guts, a good blast of music usually helped diffuse it. It was a trick he'd learned many years ago, reinforced and perfected when he'd ached with every fibre of his being to pulverise the teenage boy who'd tried to force himself on Elsa. The tautness in his guts right now felt very different from that long-ago tension.

'It's not your family in danger,' she said.

'Isn't it?'

His words hung in the enveloping silence.

A few miles later and he saw the tell-tale colours of a fast food restaurant.

'Hungry?'

'No.'

'Well, I am.'

The restaurant had a drive-through. He pulled into it and opened his window to give his order.

Minutes later and he reached for the bulging paper bag and drinks tray, passed them to Elsa who had no choice but to take them, then drove into a bay.

Taking the paper bag off her lap and putting it on his own, he then un-wedged the coffees from the tray and put them in the car's cup holders. He pulled out squares of sugar for Elsa from the bag, then removed a burger box and fries and handed them to her too.

'I said I wasn't hungry,' she said stiffly.

Unwrapping his double burger, he shrugged and took an enormous bite. 'I'll eat it if you don't want it.'

Despite her private vow to ignore him for the duration of their journey, Elsa couldn't help but notice how he devoured his food with the same appreciation he'd always shown, and found herself flooded afresh by memories. How many times had Santi collected her from parties and, in an attempt to sober her up before she had to face her parents, bought her fast food and black coffee doused with plenty of sugar?

Looking back, she could see she'd deliberately drunk too much on those nights out with her friends just so he would look after her.

When she finally looked at the food on her lap, a huge pang rippled through her heart to see it was the chicken burger she'd always favoured.

He'd remembered.

She didn't doubt he also remembered the night she'd waited in his bed for him, and as she thought that, the little appetite she'd regained by smelling the food vanished, and she handed the box to him. 'Have it.'

'With pleasure.'

Their fingers touched as he took the box and a shock of heat danced through her. Suddenly breathless and unsettled, Elsa leaned as far from him as she could and pressed her cheek against the cold window.

When he'd finished every scrap of both his meal and hers, he drove to a bin, opened his window, and dropped their rubbish into it.

And then they were off again.

'How come you ended up studying in Vienna?' Santi asked. The Autobahn stretched before them. He estimated they had another four hours of driving before they reached their first destination, and Elsa's cold silence was fast becoming intolerable. The Elsa-scented air had stopped the radio working as a distraction. Her perfume was much lighter and more subtle than the heavy, cloying fragrance she used to douse herself in. This one had a gorgeous, delicate fruity tone and his nostrils twitched to drag it deep into his lungs.

'It seemed like a nice city,' she muttered.

He worked at loosening his jaw. Everything felt tight, as if all the bones in his body had locked together. 'You were going to study in Valencia.'

'I changed my mind.'

'Why?'

Elsa closed her eyes. She didn't want conversation. Santi's voice…

She clenched her jaw tightly. Barely half a day together and already his voice, deep, gravelly, *sexy*, was doing things to her.

It was because she'd been taken so unawares, she told herself. No time to prepare for being with him. This heated, sickly tension was just a muscle memory. An echo.

She wasn't that obsessive, reckless girl any more. She walked rather than ran. She listened carefully rather than talk nineteen to the dozen. She was in control of herself. Feelings didn't dictate her actions. She considered things carefully. Impulse had no part in her life.

'I asked why you changed your mind,' Santi pressed.

From the corner of his eye he saw her raise a shoulder. 'University is supposed to broaden your horizons. Marisa kept telling me I was a fool for wanting to live at home rather than experience everything university had to offer. I decided she was right.'

'So why stay after you graduated? You were going to join the business.'

He remembered the hours she'd spent talking about the day she took her place in the family business, her excitement for the travelling and adventure that would come with it, all her ideas for it. Instead of doing the thing she'd spent her whole life looking forward to, she'd taken an office job with a Viennese recruitment company. He couldn't begin to imagine what kind of excitement recruitment gave to someone with Elsa's zest for life.

Another glimpse of shoulder rising. 'Vienna suited me.'

'How did you find the language?'

'It took a while for me to pick it up but I'm fluent now.'

'Did your Austrian boyfriend help you?' He dropped this question casually. For some unfathomable reason his heart seemed to stop while he waited the few beats for her answer.

'Which one?'

He laughed at her chutzpah. 'How many have you had?'

'Enough.'

'Your parents told me you were serious about someone called Stefan.' He reflexively tightened his grip on the wheel. 'They kept waiting for you to bring him home so they could meet him.'

'It didn't work out.'

'Why not?'

Another shoulder rise. 'We wanted different things.'

'What did you want?'

'A man who didn't keep bombarding me with questions like someone from the Inquisition,' she said pointedly.

He laughed again. 'We haven't spoken in five years. Is it a crime to want to know how you've been?'

'From what you've said, you already know everything.'

'I only know what your *mamá* has told me. She's

very proud of you. Your *papá* was too. And I know *you*, *chiquita*, and what an accomplished liar you are.'

'I am *not*.' It was the most animation he'd heard since he'd forced the conversation on her.

'Don't get defensive. People lie. Teenagers especially. It's human nature. You happen to be very good at fooling your family.'

'I'm not a teenager any more. And you lied to them too.'

'Not in words. I omitted a few things but if they had ever asked me directly, I would have told the truth. I'm glad they didn't ask. It is better for parents not to know everything their children get up to, I think.'

'I didn't do anything more or less than others my age did.'

'And that's why I never had to tell them. You experimented like all teenagers do but compared to how I behaved as a teenager, you were an angel.'

He felt her curiosity pique in the subtle way she straightened. It was a little tell he remembered from the days when they'd been as close as cousins.

'What did you get up to?'

'Stuff you wouldn't believe.' Stuff he would never have dreamed of sharing when she'd been an impressionable teenager. And stuff it shamed him to his core to remember.

'Try me.'

'Okay…' The woman beside him was no longer an impressionable teenager, he reminded himself. 'You remember the day you went cliff jumping and hurt your back?'

Elsa reluctantly allowed the memory to surface. It had been a forty-foot drop into the sea and she'd landed badly. The exhilaration as she'd flown through the air had been worth the pain. Rather than get a lift back with a friend, she'd called Santi. He'd kept his mouth shut when she'd blithely told her parents she'd hurt it after falling down some stairs. 'Yes...'

'I did the same thing at the same age but I was drunk out of my mind. I nearly drowned. I was wild, always drinking, always on the lookout for trouble, fighting anyone who looked at me the wrong way, rarely attending school and when I did it was to cause trouble. I never knew when to draw the line.'

Elsa knew boys like Santi had described. They were the kind of boys he'd always warned her about.

'I don't remember you being like that.' She couldn't remember Santi as a teenager at all. In her mind, he'd always been a man. Eleven years older than her twenty-three years, he'd been a part of her life for all her life, the long-dead housekeeper's son who'd continued to live on their estate in the cottage he'd shared with his mother, but in Elsa's younger years he'd been a shadow in the background.

By her tenth birthday he'd become her father's right-hand man, the man who occasionally picked her up from her private school or ballet lessons and occasionally joined the family for Sunday dinner; an elusive big brother with no time for pesky little girls who only wanted to talk about ballet and horses. He'd only taken solid form in her mind when she'd gone to that first unchaperoned house party and he'd turned into her unofficial chauffeur and protector.

'You were too young to have known, and in those days I was kept away from you and Marisa.' Those were the days Santi looked back on with shame and self-loathing and his knuckles tightened over the steering wheel again as the vision of his PE teacher's pulverised face flashed in his eyes. 'If not for your father, my life would have taken a very different path. He was a good man. The best. The best mentor a boy could have and, *damn*, I *miss* him.'

'I miss him too,' Elsa whispered. Her heart throbbed with the sharp pain that had rarely dulled since his death.

'I know you do.'

She closed her eyes and breathed in deeply through her nose, only to find Santi's earthy, musky scent filling her lungs.

A tear spilled down her cheek. She brushed it away and swallowed back more tears. The confines of the car were closing in on her. She didn't want to talk any more. Didn't want to think. All she wanted was to be home with her family and for this nightmare to be over.

But Santi's scent was growing in intensity, feeding the nightmare, and now she imagined she could feel the heat from his body too. 'Can we open the roof?'

'Not a good idea.'

'Why not?'

'Your hair is very distinctive.' The curse of being a redhead in a country where less than two percent of the population were naturally that colour. 'Best we don't take unnecessary risks.'

'Do you mind if I open the window then?'

'Go ahead.'

As the fresh air pooled in, she put her face to it and welcomed it into her lungs, welcomed it pushing out Santi's scent. The way her body reacted to it frightened her. It reminded her too sharply of the hunger she'd felt for him all those years ago.

That had been a hunger categorically not reciprocated.

The sun was descending when Santi parked the car. He removed his shades and checked the messages on his secure phone, then rolled his neck to loosen it and stretched his back.

Elsa had fallen asleep an hour ago. When calling her name failed to rouse her, he placed a finger on her shoulder and gently prodded it.

Her eyes flew open and locked onto his.

It had been a long time since Santi had gazed into those eyes, a curious combination of green and brown, as clear as crystal but with unfathomable depth, and as he stared, his sinews tightened.

He'd spent the day running on adrenaline, assuming the knots in his guts were caused by the situation. He'd filled the tension between them with music and conversation, never allowing himself a moment to acknowledge the beautiful woman Elsa had blossomed into. She'd always been a pretty thing but now… Oval-faced with rounded cheekbones, a cute little nose, lips shaped like Cupid's bow and long silky locks the colour of autumn leaves… Elsa was stunning. The most ravishing woman he'd seen in all his thirty-four years.

A pulse beat loudly in his head. He could only have been trapped in her gaze a matter of moments but in those moments time became elastic, stretching until he forced himself back to the present.

He cleared his throat. 'We're here.'

She blinked a number of times before turning her face and covering her mouth to hide a wide yawn.

Elsa took in her surroundings, glad to have something to focus on that wasn't Santi, glad to have a moment to settle her heart without his all too knowing gaze on her face.

He'd parked in front of an enormous log cabin situated at the base of a steep forest. Craning her neck, she caught a glimmer of water a short distance behind them. 'Where are we?'

'Carinthia,' he answered.

She knew of the popular Austrian spot with mountains and lakes, situated within the Eastern Alps but had never visited. 'You're sure we've not been followed?'

'I detected no tail. I've had a message from Felipe—the cartel know you've disappeared. They're looking for you but nothing in their communications suggests they're close.' His teeth flashed. 'They think you took the train.'

'Good.' She gave another yawn and looked again at the picturesque lodge. 'I'm guessing the cartel won't expect us to stay in a holiday resort?'

'Who knows what they think? But this isn't a holiday resort. I own it.'

That shocked her. Santi had bought a property in *Austria*? 'Since when?'

He shrugged. 'I bought it as an investment last year under a business name. The lake's on the doorstep and in the winter it's within easy reach of the ski resorts, so should be popular with summer vacationers and winter sports enthusiasts. I've had a team renovating it. Luckily for us, the renovations were completed a couple of weeks ago.' He opened his door. 'Come on. Let's get inside.'

Elsa got out. Absolute silence filled her ears, not even a rustle of breeze disturbing the stillness.

The beauty of the setting made her heart sigh. It was as if nature had carved a secret horseshoe into the verdant terrain for the lake to fill, the lodge hidden beneath the forest from prying eyes. She pictured it in winter: the lake frozen, the roof of the lodge and the tall trees and mountains thick with snow. Magical.

She turned and found Santi removing cases from the boot of the car.

Her heart swelled and caught in her throat.

Why had he chosen this spot? Why here, in Austria?

Five years before she'd left Valencia, he'd set up his own business. By the time she'd left, it had grown into a billion-euro venture. She'd barely noticed his growing wealth because nothing had changed between them. He was still just Santi.

In the five years she'd lived in Vienna, his wealth had grown to such an extent she could barely comprehend the figures. It seemed like every conversation with her mother involved a brief telling of his latest acquisition. Rosaria's pride rang in her voice. The years Elsa had been away, his business had turned into an empire. Santi had the Midas touch, and when she followed him up the steps and into the lodge, she found the interior worthy of King Midas himself.

Walking beneath high, oak-beamed ceilings and over gleaming oak floor covered with numerous exquisite rugs, she soaked everything in. The last of the day's light poured in through the plentiful high windows and bounced over highly expensive furniture that was both luxurious and inviting.

'Is this really a holiday let?' she asked, already awestruck despite having seen only a fraction of the lodge. If this was hers, she'd want to keep it all for herself and her family.

He ran his fingers through his black slicked-back hair and nodded.

'I'm guessing it's for an elite clientele,' she murmured, her attention now captured by a carved oak table placed in a nook that had a map of the world inlaid in marble on its round top.

'It's for those who can afford it. There's eight bedrooms upstairs. Take your pick, they're all made up. Dinner's been delivered and is keeping warm in the kitchen, so follow your nose when you're hungry. Explore. Use whatever facilities you wish, just bear in mind there's no staff here at the moment.'

As he spoke, Santi edged away from her in the direction of the stairs. She told herself she didn't care that he obviously couldn't wait for some distance from her. *She* couldn't wait for some respite from *him*.

'We'll be leaving early in the morning so relax and get some sleep,' he continued. 'I'll leave your case upstairs for you.'

'*My* case?' In all the day's drama, she'd forgotten she didn't have any spare clothes with her.

'Your sister packed it for you. The phone I told you about is in it. You can call your family but no one else. There's also a wig in there.'

Her heart sank. Marisa's taste in clothes differed greatly from Elsa's. Her big sister liked to tease her about how conservatively she now dressed, as if there was something wrong with stylish jeans and pretty tops, and knee-length skirts and dresses.

'What's the wig for?'

'I told you, your hair's distinctive. You'll need to hide it under the wig or a hat when we're in public.'

Then he picked the cases up and, without another word, disappeared with them.

CHAPTER THREE

BY GOD'S GRACE and spacious accommodation, Santi managed to avoid Elsa for the rest of the evening.

It proved impossible to avoid her presence, though. Barely a day in her company and he felt more wired and on edge than he'd felt since...

Since those torturous days after he'd found her in his bed.

To keep his mind occupied and far from Elsa, and to pass the hours before he slept, he checked in on his business and satisfied himself that there weren't any serious issues that needed his attention.

It had been many years since he'd taken time away from the business he'd formed a decade ago. Santi had had the idea of starting a complementary business to the Lopezes' shipping one, a fleet of airliners that were exclusively for the transportation of goods. He'd picked up a lot of knowledge through his work as Marco's right-hand man and had saved virtually all the money he'd earned from him. He'd been ready to strike out on his own.

Marco, as was his generous nature, had been more

than happy to guide him. He'd willingly shared his contacts and office space, and invested a chunk of his own money in Santi's venture. They'd worked as closely together as they'd done since Marco had bailed him out that final time. Five years later, all the investment had been repaid and Santi's business had started to make a killing.

The same week Elsa had left home for Vienna, Santi had moved out of the housekeeper's cottage, which they'd insisted he could live in for ever if he wanted, and into a villa he'd had built a kilometre away. He'd moved his arthritic grandmother from her cramped fourth-floor apartment in Seville into a spacious ground-floor one in an exclusive retirement complex. He'd bought himself a fleet of cars. He'd commissioned a two-hundred-foot super-yacht. He'd bought himself an apartment in New York, a penthouse in Milan and a three-storey house in London, the last of which he was still to spend a night in. This Austrian lodge was just one of many business investments he'd poured his money into.

His success would have been dizzying if he'd had time to think about it but he was always busy working, expanding and micromanaging the business, investing in new ventures…

Far from enjoying the fruits of his labour, he'd become a workaholic. Long, lazy lunches followed by relaxing siestas became a thing of the past. Long, lazy evening meals with good company followed by dancing in smoky clubs until the early hours had been similarly eschewed. For five years Santi had done nothing but work.

One day, when the time was right, he would board his yacht—since delivery, he'd used it once, for entertaining purposes—and sail the Caribbean. He hoped to have found a wife by then. Maybe have a few children. The days of feeling imaginary shackles on his wrists and ankles at the thought of marriage had long gone, but how could a man like him find a wife? Overnight, he'd gone from playing the field with relish to rarely dating. The few lovers he'd had in the past five years had been fleeting affairs that had satisfied nothing more than his basic needs.

That this morph into workaholism had coincided with Elsa's move to Vienna was pure coincidence. That he'd bought this lodge in the country she'd chosen to base her life was coincidence too.

Infuriated that he was *still* thinking of her and certain his brain was too wired for sleep, he decided to take a swim and work some of the tension out of his body.

Grabbing his swim-shorts, he padded quietly past the room Elsa had picked for herself, and headed down to the ground floor spa.

The room Elsa had selected was so elegant and beautiful that, if she hadn't been so desperate to get home to her family, she'd have loved to spend more than a night in it.

A pang rent her chest to imagine spending time here over winter with her family, enjoying the white Christmas she and Marisa had dreamed of as children. The picture came fully formed. Her. Marisa. Baby Nikos. Their mother. Their father. Santi…

No mental image of her family came complete without Santi.

But it was picturing her dead father that turned the pang into a deep, tearing wrench and, aching to hear a familiar loved voice, she snatched up the phone Santi had given her and called Marisa.

Just hearing her sister's voice was enough to soothe her. When Marisa put the phone on loudspeaker so Elsa could talk to their mother and hear baby Nikos babbling away, her chest loosened enough for her to breathe properly. Once she was satisfied that the three people she loved most in the world were safe, she lay back on the sleigh bed and closed her eyes. Santi's face swam before her.

Frustrated at her brain's inability to switch off, even more frustrated it seemed to be locked on everything Santi, she threw the covers back and rummaged through her case for one of the swimsuits she'd spotted earlier.

Thankfully, the clothes Marisa had packed *were* Elsa's own…mostly. Marisa had also packed a couple of her own dresses. They exposed way too much flesh, especially around the cleavage and thighs. Under no circumstances would she wear them, especially not around Santi, not when the disgust that had oozed from him all those years ago still plagued her. Overnight, she'd gone from being a body-confident young woman to someone who could hardly bring herself to look at her naked reflection.

She changed into the swimsuit then slipped on the towelling robe hanging in the bathroom and secured it tightly before creeping out of the room and tiptoeing down the stairs.

During her solitary tour of the lodge earlier, she'd found a vast spa facility on the lower ground floor, but she'd only given it a cursory glance, too on edge about bumping into *him*, before finding her dinner in the rustic kitchen and taking it to her room, where she'd intended to hide until morning.

She hadn't had the chance to fully appreciate the spa's breathtaking glory earlier. She appreciated it now. Completely different in tone and feel from the rest of the lodge, its marble flooring and ornate pillars made her think of Roman baths from millennia ago. So taken was she by the life-sized marble statues lining the walls of the swimming area that it took her a beat to notice the human figure climbing out of the water at the far end of the vast pool.

Santi.

Her abdomen clenched then released in ripples.

Oblivious to her presence, he leaned over to snatch a towel from a lounging chair and rubbed it over his face.

Her heartbeats echoed in her ears. Even if he'd noticed her there, at that moment she wouldn't have been able to react. Her feet were rooted to the floor. The magnificent torso, all hard muscle with a smattering of dark hair across the pecs that had fascinated her from the age of fifteen, was *right there*, only the gold chain with an attached cross he'd worn for as long as she could remember and a pair of swim-shorts on his skin.

Dimly, she remembered Marisa's eighteen birthday. Their parents had thrown a pool party at the villa to celebrate. The sun had shone brightly. Everyone had been there, a melding of generations all having fun, diving in and out of the pool, eating barbecued meats, drinking cocktails and singing along to cheesy party tunes. Elsa and her friends Carmen and Lola, all of sixteen but trying desperately to act like adults, had stretched out on sunbeds and ogled Santi from behind their huge sunglasses.

Santi had been the one to notice when she'd helped herself to her third margarita. Wearing only a pair of swim-shorts, his glorious body damp from the pool as it was now, he'd plucked it from her hand, shaken his head with an indulgent smile, then grooved his way back to the pool, drinking her cocktail.

If she hadn't been so breathless at the accidental brush of his finger against hers when he'd pilfered her drink, she would have been furious.

She was breathless now too.

He turned slightly and froze.

Despite the distance of the pool between them, their eyes clashed. Held.

Eyes not leaving Elsa's face, Santi slowly lifted the towel to his head and rubbed it over his hair.

Whatever good his vigorous swim had done had been shattered in an instant. Caught unawares, no time to shield his thoughts or responses, awareness rippled through him like a riptide.

Her trim, slender body was hidden behind an enormous robe but his heated blood flowed as if she were wearing provocative lingerie.

The image he'd spent five years doing his damnedest to suppress flashed through him. Elsa. Naked on his bed...

He slammed the memory shut.

As if she were privy to his mental turmoil, Elsa suddenly reared back. Her gaze held his for barely another beat before she turned around.

Santi expelled a slow breath and closed his eyes. When he opened them, she'd gone.

Were it not for the arousal filling him so painfully, he would believe he'd imagined her.

Elsa gripped the bannister tightly as she descended the stairs early the next morning.

She refused to think about why facing Santi should make her stomach feel as if it was in a milk churn and her heart thump loudly.

Why did she have to dream about him? Wasn't it enough that he'd pushed himself to the forefront of her mind so that every time she closed her eyes his face was there before her without invading her dreams too?

It had to be that brief late-night moment by the pool. A brief moment that had passed like an eternity.

It's just an echo, she told herself stubbornly. All of

it. An echo from the days when she'd been obsessed with him.

That echo reverberated through her now as she followed the scent of bacon to the kitchen, becoming violent when she found him spreading butter over thick slices of bread.

He looked up as she entered and flashed the familiar, easy-going smile that made the lines around his eyes crinkle. 'Good morning, *chiquita*. I'm making bacon sandwiches if you want one? Not quite a full English breakfast but we need to hit the road soon.'

The thought of food made her stomach roil. Santi's good humour and nonchalance while she'd spent hours torturing herself over her growing unrequited awareness landed like barbed wire on her skin. There was not a single sign that *he'd* spent the evening torturing himself, she thought bitterly. And why would he? What had she ever meant to him other than as his mentor's daughter? Whatever she thought she'd detected in his eyes in unguarded moments were echoes too of the time when her feverish imagination had been desperate to believe her feelings were reciprocated.

'I'm not hungry,' she said curtly, not looking at him as she walked to the coffee pot.

A sugar pot swished over the counter and came to a stop beside the mug he'd left out for her.

'Help yourself to extra sugar,' Santi said, his efforts at good humour gone. 'It might sweeten you up.'

Far from a good night's sleep brightening Elsa's mood, she seemed as hostile as she'd been yesterday.

Under the circumstances, he didn't expect her to be carefree and light, but she was making little effort to hide her antagonism and it was becoming more and more obvious that it was directed at him and not the situation.

Could she be holding a grudge from that night? He'd hurt her when he'd rejected her, he knew that. He'd had to.

She would never know how much he'd hurt himself too.

He took the two sandwiches he'd made for himself and the one he'd made for Elsa to the kitchen table and took his first bite. Definitely not as good as a full English, a feast he'd discovered years ago after partying all night at a British stag party and then joining them for breakfast, but enough to stave off the hunger pangs.

By the time he'd eaten the first, his anger had quelled a little. He kept his gaze fixed on the lake view from the window. He would not look at her again until he was certain he had his emotions under control. It didn't help that she was dressed in a pretty knee-length red floral wrap dress that hugged her slender body sensually.

How the hell did she evoke such wildly disparate emotions in him? She should elicit nothing but platonic familiarity. He should *not* be sitting there fighting the stirring in his loins, fighting his own mind from mentally undressing her. He didn't care that Elsa was a fully-grown woman now. She was forbidden fruit. She would always be forbidden fruit.

But he hated this tension. Hated to feel his muscles

bunch together as if priming for a fight. The fight, he knew, was against himself.

When she broke the silence by quietly asking, 'Where's the road taking us today?' he made sure to keep his voice and features neutral with his reply.

'Portofino.'

'Isn't that in Italy?'

He nodded. 'If we leave within the hour, we should be there by sundown.'

'How many kilometres is it?'

'About seven hundred.'

'We're going to do the trip in one go?'

'The sooner we're at sea, the better.'

As Elsa was in complete agreement about that, she headed to the door. 'I'll get my stuff together.'

It was a relief to leave the kitchen. The scent of bacon was too reminiscent of the days when Santi would take her out for breakfast. Say what you like about English food, their traditional breakfast was amazing. The first time she'd had one had been after he'd picked her up from a sleepover at Lola's house. That had been an extra-special delight because she hadn't been expecting him. Her mum was supposed to collect her, but she'd double-booked herself with her hairdresser and asked Santi if he could get her instead.

Thinking back on it, she was certain he'd taken her to that café because he'd had a hangover. It had never occurred to Elsa that he might have had other plans for that Saturday morning, plans that had included sleeping.

Was this what the rest of their trip would be like?

she wondered miserably as she climbed the stairs. Wave after wave of forgotten memories punching her?

Back in her room, she went to the bathroom and pinned her hair to the crown of her head and carefully put the chin-length brown wig on. If she wore it for the car journey, she'd be able to put the car's roof down and not have Santi's cologne invade her airwaves. She could take it off once they were at sea on his luxury yacht. With its five decks, ample cabins and large crew, she would have the space to hide away from him until they reached Valencia.

A loud knock on her door set her pulses racing and then Santi's handsome, rugged face appeared. A slight frown appeared on his brow as he took in the wig but he made no comment about it and made no effort to enter her room. 'Are you ready?'

She nodded and slung her bag over her shoulder.

An hour after leaving the lodge, they crossed the border into Italy. Santi was confident they had no tail.

Soon, surrounded by Alpine mountains, they entered the Canal Valley town of Tarvisio. He drove them straight to a hotel with an unobserved car park where he pulled up beside a Maserati GranTurismo. The fob for it was nestled behind the driver's wheel.

Elsa said not a single word while they made the switch.

She hadn't said a voluntary word since they'd left.

'Can you work the radio for me?' he asked when they were back on the autostrada.

In silence, she complied. In no time they were listening to an American singer wailing an upbeat tune about her rotten bunch of previous lovers. It did nothing to ease the tension he could feel in his every sinew. Every inhalation dragged Elsa's light fruity scent into his lungs. God help him but the urge to lean into her and inhale deeply was growing by the second.

He gritted his teeth. Music wasn't working. He needed a distraction.

'Tell me about Stefan,' he commanded.

'Why?'

'Just making conversation.' Although why he wanted details of her old lover as a distraction was something he didn't know. Santi pictured Stefan in his mind, one of those strait-laced men who'd excelled in school academically and on the sports field, and had as much personality as a bucket of paint.

'Can't we make conversation about something else?'

'It ended on a bad note, did it?' he guessed, pitching his tone at cheerful. When she refused to answer, he added, 'You know, we're going to be together for a long time. You can't keep ignoring me.'

'I can.'

He laughed. 'You'll never keep it up. You were always such a chatterbox.'

'I'm not that girl any more.'

That much he did know. Elsa had changed. The springy girlishness she'd oozed had been replaced with something far more self-contained.

'Then tell me who you are now. What does the grown-up Elsa Lopez like to do?'

'She likes to go for walks and spinning classes, read books and watch boxsets.'

'But does she still party like it's going out of fashion? Is she still the Queen Bee amongst a large circle of friends?'

'I was never Queen Bee.'

'You were,' he contradicted. 'Your friends flocked around you. You couldn't go anywhere in the villa or the grounds without tripping over a teenage girl.'

'That's because they all fancied you.'

'What?'

'Don't pretend you didn't know.'

'How would I have known that? I was old enough to be their...'

'Big brother,' she supplied drily. 'And they all fancied the pants off you.'

'Teenage girls are not my thing,' he dismissed. He'd noticed them—he'd have had to be blind not to, otherwise he really would have tripped over them—but never as females to be pursued. He liked his women to be women, not giggling banshees.

'You made that abundantly clear,' Elsa muttered.

She only realised she'd said the words aloud when he replied, 'If you're talking about the night I found you in my bed then—'

The old mortification rushed through her. 'I don't want to talk about that,' she interrupted.

'We *need* to talk about it.'

'I was drunk. I barely remember it.' Remembering how drunk she'd been was mortifying too. She'd helped herself to her mother's rum for courage then, when her nerve had almost deserted her, helped herself to a little more.

If only she'd drunk enough to forget everything about that night. Instead, it was stained in her memories. The night her heart had broken and her dreams had died.

'Really?' he asked sceptically.

'You can't think I actually *fancied* you? You were far too old for me.'

'Then you should thank me for not taking advantage of you,' he retorted. 'Some men might get their kicks from sleeping with drunken virgins but I'm not one of them.'

Elsa wanted to cover her face from the flames of humiliation his words provoked.

What a fool she'd been to think Santi had been waiting for her to come of age. She'd spent her eighteenth birthday on tenterhooks, waiting for the moment he declared his love for her as she'd spent three years fantasising, only to go to bed after her party disappointed. But then, the very next morning, in the villa's kitchen, she'd seen something in his eyes that had made her heart leap, a look that had consumed her for hours until she'd become convinced that Santi was waiting for *her* to declare herself.

The idea had bloomed as the day had gone on. Panic had already been building over his imminent move from his cottage on the Lopez estate to a newly built ten-bedroom villa a kilometre away.

She'd cycled past the construction site of his villa many times, plotting ways to sabotage the build and keep him with her for longer, until it had occurred to her that sabotage was unnecessary—he must be waiting for her to turn eighteen before asking her to move in with him!

Well, if he wanted her to move in with him, he needed to hurry up about it. Her pathetic little brain had decided that it must be shyness or old-fashioned chivalry preventing him admitting his feelings. She'd *had* to act. The best part of a bottle of rum had greatly aided this mind-set. Declaring her love had been the only logical course of action.

If she could go back in time and stop herself entering his cottage that night, she would.

The morning after, she'd wanted to crawl into a hole and die.

Remembering the anguish…oh, it was all coming back to her in unvarnished colour. The cruel things he'd said. The look on his face as he'd said them…

'Thank you for not taking advantage of me,' she said as coldly as she could manage with her heart being wrenched into pieces and the old worthlessness and shame sitting heavily in her stomach.

'I'm sorry if I hurt you that night. I never—'

'You didn't hurt me. It was a drunken mistake and I don't want to waste another breath talking about it. In fact, I don't want to talk about anything so if you don't mind, let's skip playing getting-to-know-each-other-again. I don't *want* to know you. All I want is to get home to my family.'

Santi had to force his knuckles to loosen on the steering wheel. He had to force his jaw to loosen too. Elsa's tone told him quite clearly that she hated him. 'If I didn't hurt you, why all the hostility?'

'I *said* I don't want to talk about it.' To accentuate her point, she turned the radio up so high the sound pierced straight through him.

'Cut it out,' Santi snarled, turning it down. 'Are you trying to make me crash?'

'Just stop *talking*!' she suddenly screamed, her voice as ear-splitting as the radio had been.

'What the hell is wrong with you?' he demanded.

'*You* are what's wrong with me.'

His fingers tightened on the wheel again. 'Very mature.'

She mumbled something under her breath that he couldn't make out and folded her arms tightly across her chest. He didn't have to see her face to imagine the defiant expression on it, which only added to his anger at her attitude and behaviour.

'Spend the rest of our journey sulking all you like,' he said, 'but if you pull another stunt like you just did with the volume, I'll chuck you in the boot. Understand?'

'I'd like to see you try.'

'Would you really?'

'Oh, do one,' she muttered mutinously, shifting to lean against the door.

Clamping his teeth together, he pushed the roof control button and in what felt like seconds, the roof disappeared and warm, fresh air blew around his face. It did nothing to blow his anger away.

And then he caught a glimpse of Elsa's dark wig blowing in the breeze and his heart ached to remember the reason she was wearing it.

Once, they had been friends. Good friends. Elsa had been his little buddy. He couldn't have been more protective of her if she'd been of his blood.

And then one day he'd looked at her and everything had changed.

CHAPTER FOUR

THE CHANGE HAD come the morning after Elsa's eighteenth birthday. Santi had gone into the villa to collect some paperwork he'd needed her father's signature on. She'd been at the breakfast bar, clutching her head, dressed in a thin pink robe.

'Hangover?' he'd asked without an ounce of sympathy. Her parents had thrown a pool party for her, just as they'd done for her sister. Unlike at Marisa's party, Santi hadn't needed to police Elsa's alcohol consumption since she had technically become an adult.

She'd groaned and got to her feet. 'Can you take me for an English breakfast?'

'Sorry, *chiquita*, but I've got a full day ahead of me. Tomorrow?'

'I'll try not to have a hangover for it.'

He'd grinned.

Her green-tinged face had managed a small smile in return before she'd staggered to the kitchen door. Morning light had pooled in through the vast windows and suddenly illuminated her.

His throat had run dry.

The light illuminating her slender frame had made the robe transparent. Elsa had clearly been naked beneath it.

And then she'd turned around, walked back to the breakfast bar for her phone, mumbling something under her breath, oblivious to the fact that Santi had been able to see *everything*.

Less than twenty-four hours earlier he'd watched Elsa dance around the pool in nothing but a skimpy bikini and felt not the slightest stir of arousal. His mind and body had never gone there.

Their eyes had met. There had been a breathless feeling in his chest, as if his lungs had been slowly collapsing. He'd been unable to tear his gaze from her.

It had felt like he was seeing her for the first time, seeing her as a woman...

Desire had pooled deep within him, hot and thick, as disturbing for the depth of its intensity as for the object of his sudden craving.

His departure had been abrupt and he'd driven away from the villa in turmoil, unable to rid himself of the image of Elsa's naked silhouette. He'd arrived at the mammoth new warehousing complex he'd had built next to his airfield and ironed out the issues his manager had identified, all the while wishing he could scrub his eyes clean. Then Marco had turned up to sign the documents and the guilt had hit him like a truck.

If Marco or Rosaria knew Santi desired their youngest daughter...

They would have been horrified. And he wouldn't

have blamed them. The cruellest thing, though, was that it wouldn't be the age gap that would bother them, Marco being ten years older than Rosaria. He, Santi, was just not good enough. He might have built himself a thriving business and a small fortune but the new trappings of his life didn't change his humble beginnings. It didn't change who he was inside. It didn't change the fact he'd once put a teacher in hospital with his fists and that if Marco hadn't stepped in, Santi would have gone to prison for it.

Marco's quietly delivered decade-old words had echoed loudly in his ears that day. 'I can't do this again, Santiago. One more incident like this and I'm sorry but I'll have to ask you to leave. It would break my heart but I need to think of the girls.'

It had been the final warning after Santi had put the Lopezes through three years of hell. He would never forget the sorrow and disappointment that had been reflected in Marco's eyes. That, more than anything, had been the impetus for Santi to make the behavioural changes so desperately needed.

What kind of man would he be to repay everything Marco had given him, which *was* everything, by falling for his daughter? The Lopezes were good people who wanted their daughters to make good marriages with good, clean-living men.

That night, Santi had returned late to his cottage and found Elsa in his bed.

It was five years ago, he reminded himself grimly, refusing to think about that night. The past. History.

He turned the radio up to a not quite ear-splitting level and drowned the past out with music.

Three hours later Santi drove into an exclusive gated road and stopped in the underground car park of a sprawling medieval home that had once belonged to nobility but now belonged to an acquaintance he'd got to know at a private members' club. The acquaintance in question had used Felipe Lorenzi's services himself and was completely trustworthy.

'Why have we stopped?' Elsa asked. They were the first words either had spoken since their earlier bitter exchange.

'Food,' he replied shortly. 'There's a decent coffee shop close by. If you're not hungry, you can watch me eat.'

Elsa practically jumped out. The lowering of the car roof had done nothing to stop her lungs filling with Santi-scented air.

After hours spent in the car, it felt good to stretch her legs.

As they walked the narrow streets lined with centuries-old buildings, Elsa had the sense of walking into the past. She wished she could explore properly. In the five years she'd lived in Vienna, she'd explored every inch of it on foot. She liked to walk. It was a good way to clear her mind and bring herself to a state of calm. At least, it had been before her father's death. Since then there had been too many shadows for any kind of peace.

Five minutes after they'd left the car, she followed Santi into a small but crowded café.

'We can't spend too long in here so I'm going to have a panini,' he said, having to lean in close to make himself heard over the bustle of chatter coming from all directions. 'What do you want?'

She looked at the chalkboard menu at the back of the serving counter. 'A mozzarella and prosciutto panini, please.'

'Coffee?'

She nodded and cast her gaze around for a table. A pair of elderly gentlemen were rising from a corner one, and she indicated to Santi that she would try and get it for them. When no one else tried to claim it, she quickly parked her bottom on the closest chair. She leaned back and let the warm, friendly atmosphere infuse her.

'You've lost your frown lines,' Santi observed when he joined her. He took the seat she'd placed her bag on to stop anyone else using it, and placed a couple of bottles of water on the table.

'It's nice to have a moment of normality,' she admitted wistfully, but the brief inner peace she'd found was over even as she spoke, the café so crowded that Santi was forced to shuffle his chair right next to hers to accommodate his massive frame.

Their coffees and paninis were brought to them.

Painfully aware of Santi's closeness, Elsa kept her elbows as tight to her sides as she could. Their thighs were a hair's breadth from brushing together and no matter how hard she tried to ignore him, her skin seemed to be inhaling the heat from his muscular body the way a plant breathed in sunlight.

God, but her heart was jumping all over the place. Her stomach had tightened too but she forced the food down her throat. She must keep her strength up. And, though she tried her hardest to keep her eyes averted, she was still so *aware* of him. He'd devoured his panini before she'd eaten a quarter of hers.

His appetite was something that had once fascinated her. His appetite was *huge*, and not only for food. Life for Santi had been something to be lived to the full. The only aspect of it she'd tried hard not to think about was his appetite for women. She couldn't remember a single meal they'd shared that hadn't been interrupted by some woman or other calling or messaging him. Whenever she'd slyly asked if she needed to buy a wedding hat, he'd put his wrists together as if they were cuffed and give the most exaggerated shudder.

She'd dreaded the day he confided that there was a woman he was becoming serious about. He was supposed to be waiting for her!

Had he found a woman to settle down with? For all she knew, he might have spent the past five years living with someone. But he hadn't married or had children, that much she knew with confidence. If Santi ever married, her mother would be guest of honour. If he had children, her mother would be godmother.

Elsa had once believed, with the naïve self-absorption teenagers pulled off so well, that when Santi married her mother would be mother of the bride, and that when he had children her mother would be their grandmother.

Why was she thinking like this? What good did it

do to remember how deeply her obsession of him had infected her?

And why did she feel like crying?

Shoving her chair back, she grabbed her bag and got hurriedly to her feet.

'Where are you going?' he asked.

Already walking, she called over her shoulder, 'To the ladies'.'

Alone in the bathroom, there was a moment of shock when she saw the dark-haired woman staring back in the mirror. She wished she could rip the wig off her head and stamp on it.

How was it that she was on the run from the cartel who'd killed her father and instead of looking over her shoulder like a frightened rabbit and fretting about her family, all her thoughts and feelings were consumed with Santi?

The walk back to the car went quickly and with the silence that had characterised their existence together since their hateful exchange earlier. They had hours and hours of travelling left, hours to be endured next to Santi with nothing to distract her. He opened the driver's door and was about to climb in when Elsa was struck by an impulse.

'Why don't I drive for a while?'

He raised a brow.

She bristled at the look. 'I know how to drive. I passed first time.'

He held his hands up for peace. 'I was surprised at the offer, that's all.'

'We've still got four hundred kilometres to cover if we're going to make it to Portofino by evening. I can share the load.'

He raised his other brow. 'Have you driven a car as powerful as this before?'

She narrowed her eyes. 'I hope you're not implying that I'm incapable of driving it?'

'I wouldn't dream of it. I'm thinking only that we want to get to Portofino before the sun comes back up again.'

Lips pursed, she held her hand out for the fob.

With obvious reluctance, he dropped it into her waiting palm. She closed her fingers around it, passed her bag to him, then got behind the wheel.

Santi put the bottled water in the glove box, sent up a silent prayer and fastened his seat belt. He remembered Marco telling him with complete bemusement four years ago that Elsa had passed her driving test in Vienna, even though she had no intention of getting a car. He was about to give her some basic instructions when she turned the engine on, put the car into Reverse, did a U-turn with the smoothness of a seasoned pro, and drove out of the vast garage.

Then she stopped, turned her face to his, smiled sweetly, and said, 'Do you want to give me directions or shall we use the satnav?'

'I'll give directions.'

'Great.' Then she cackled. 'Hold tight.'

Elsa carefully nudged the car into the traffic and joined the throng leaving the city. By the time they'd crawled their way back onto the autostrada, Santi was breathing easier…right until the moment she put her foot down.

'Whoa!' he shouted. 'What's the hurry?'

In answer, she threw her head back and laughed with complete exhilaration, throwing him back in time to the days when Elsa had embraced life and thrilled at adventure. She'd been born with a thrill-seeking gene, he'd long ago come to realise. Nothing scared her. He guessed that's why she'd waited in his bed for him, just another thrill to be explored.

Understandably, that Elsa had been missing these last few days, but she was with him now. Down the fast lane she zoomed, overtaking car after car, the hair of her wig blowing behind her and the biggest smile on her face. Even with his stomach dropping with the same effect as if he were on a rollercoaster, Santi couldn't help but wish it was Elsa's beautiful natural hair blowing around her.

'Since when have you been a racer?' he asked when his stomach had settled enough for him to speak.

'My employer took us to the Nürburgring six months ago for a team-building day. I *loved* it. I haven't driven since,' she added regretfully.

He shook his head in amazement. 'You're a natural.'

'That's what the guy running the event said.' Elsa laughed again as she remembered the only good day since her father's death. 'Lots of my colleagues play racing games on their consoles. Their faces when I got the fastest lap of the day was the *best*. Beaten by a girl!'

'Very wounding to the male ego.'

'And very satisfying to the female one.'

'Why haven't you driven since?'

'I don't need to. My work's a ten-minute walk from my apartment.' But the temptation to buy herself a little sports car after that team-building day had been almost irresistible. The *rush* she'd felt...

It was a rush and a temptation she'd quickly put to one side as she'd settled back into her calm, safe life.

Seeing the traffic ahead of them was gridlocked, she slowed down.

'Other than sulking when they're beaten by a girl, what are your colleagues like?' Santi asked, after she'd brought the car to a stop. Driving had done Elsa good, he decided. She had colour on her cheeks and was answering his questions without any sense of hostility. He considered it progress.

'They're okay. It's a good company to work for.' Even though they weren't going anywhere—lights twinkling in the distance signified the stalled traffic was due to an accident—she kept both hands on the wheel. The nails that used to be manicured and painted weekly were now bare and kept to a functional length rather than resembling talons.

'You enjoy it?'

Her mouth made a funny little swirling motion while she considered her answer. It was a motion so familiar and yet from such a distant time that his heart tugged to see it.

'It's a good job,' she eventually said. 'Generous pay. Lots of perks. Lots of potential to progress up the ranks.'

'You socialise much with your colleagues?'

Her mouth pulled in. 'Not really. Can I have a bottle of water, please?'

Recognising she'd deliberately changed the subject but figuring he had plenty of time to discover her real reasons, he opened the glove box and pulled out one of the bottles.

'What the hell is that?' she suddenly squeaked.

'What?' He closed the glove box and held the water out to her, which she ignored.

'In the glove box. Please tell me it isn't a gun.'

'You want me to lie?'

'Oh, God, it *is* a gun?' She unclipped her seat belt and leaned over him to wrench the glove box open, then immediately reared back as if she'd been scalded. '*Why?* What the hell possessed you to bring a gun? My God, Santi, are you trying to get us arrested? What if we get pulled over by the police...? Look ahead of us! There's emergency lights flashing everywhere!'

'It's perfectly legal,' he assured her.

'It is *not* legal to carry a gun!'

'I have a special permit, so chill, okay?'

She ripped her sunglasses off and eyeballed him wildly. '*Chill?* That's a *gun!*'

'It's for your protection.'

'I don't want a gun protecting me!'

'So if the cartel find us, you expect me to use *what* to protect you? A water pistol?'

'I don't know!' She slammed her hands against the

steering wheel and accidentally hit the horn, making them both jump.

She put her hands back to wheel and curled her fingers around it, straightening her back, taking deep breaths in through her nose, clearly trying to regain her composure.

'Do you know how to use that thing?' she asked in a tight voice.

'Yes.'

'And would you use it?'

'Without hesitation.' Seeing the way her throat moved, he sighed. 'It's nothing but a precaution. I don't expect to use it but if the unexpected happens, I'll be ready.'

'We get into trouble and you'll shoot our way out of it?'

'We don't expect it to come to that. All the signs so far indicate that the cartel has no idea where you are and our plan is working. Felipe Lorenzi has excellent inside intelligence. His team will know when the cartel know and warn us immediately.'

'What if they can't warn us?'

'I can communicate with Felipe's team in a number of ways. The moment I send the signal, a team will be sent to us.'

'What if they can't get to us in time?'

Hating to see the fear that had gripped her, Santi dropped the bottle of water and prised her hand off the steering wheel. He held it tightly, not speaking until she turned her face to him.

'If you want me to tell you exactly how we've co-ordinated everything to protect you then I will, but it will take until we arrive in Portofino to go through it in detail. Just know this—for as long as I draw breath, nothing will happen to you.'

Something flickered in the green-brown depths of her eyes.

'When your *papá* was killed... I cannot tell you the guilt I felt that I wasn't there to save him.'

Tears formed from nowhere and glistened in her eyes. 'There was nothing you could have done,' she whispered hoarsely.

'My head knows that but my heart...' He placed her hand to his chest and tightened his grip. 'I didn't know about the cartel. I'd been working in the US, expanding my business, when it all happened. Your parents didn't tell me because they didn't want to worry me. They should have told me. I would have dropped everything in a heartbeat to get back to them.'

She swallowed and croaked, 'That's why they didn't tell you.'

'I know, and it doesn't make me feel any better. If I'd known...' He breathed deeply and brushed a finger down her cheek, felt her quiver at his touch. His face inched closer to hers as he stared intently into the green-brown pools. 'I can't change the past. God knows, I wish I could but I can't. But when I stood by your father's grave at his funeral, I swore that I would do everything in my power to keep the rest of you safe.' And, he remembered with a deep pang, that he'd been looking at

Elsa when he'd made that silent vow. 'I was the one who hired Felipe to protect you all, and over the last year he and his men have trained me.'

Confusion flashed in her eyes.

'They trained me in the techniques needed to be an effective bodyguard.'

The hand enveloped in his against his chest squeezed. 'You knew the cartel would come for us again?'

He found his gaze drawn to her Cupid's bow mouth. Their faces were so close he could feel the vibrations of her skin and inhale the sweetness of her breath.

His voice dropped to a whisper. 'I knew only that if anyone came for any of you again that I would be prepared, and I swear to you now, as God is my witness, that I will *never* let anything happen to you.'

He heard her hitched intake of breath. Saw the anguish in her eyes...and something else. Something darker. It drew him in. Hypnotised him. Made his veins and skin buzz...

Moisture filled his mouth. His lips tingled. His loins tightened. He could feel the vibrations of *his* skin pulling him to her.

He closed his eyes, senses filling with her delicate fragrance and the underlying warm scent of her skin. The tightening in his loins became a throb as their lips whispered together...

A long blare of a horn behind them had them simultaneously release their clasped hands and rear away from each other.

CHAPTER FIVE

ELSA BLINKED FRANTICALLY and put her trembling hands back on the steering wheel, holding it so tightly she felt it could easily snap. Her heart thumped so hard she feared it would burst out of her chest.

Nothing had happened, she told herself desperately, trying even more desperately to get air into her lungs. They hadn't been a breath away from kissing. It was just a moment between two people who'd lost someone they'd both loved. Nothing more. A moment of pure emotion.

But not until she'd inched the car forward to fill the small gap that had opened in front of them could she whisper, 'They didn't tell me either.'

'What?'

She would not allow her imagination to believe Santi's voice had a dazed quality to it.

'My parents.' She sucked in another breath and fought for vocal strength. For *any* kind of strength. 'About the cartel. They didn't want to worry me or make me feel guilt into returning home.' Only Marisa, who'd been working for the family business by then, had been told, and she'd been sworn to secrecy. Her devastated mother had explained everything when Elsa had arrived back home after her father's death.

Hot tears suddenly threatening to fall, Elsa blinked frantically, groped in her lap for her sunglasses and clumsily shoved them on.

How badly she wished her parents had confided in Santi. He would have seen in an instant that the protection they'd placed around themselves had been inadequate.

For all the guilt she and Santi shared for not being there, it was nothing on her mother's guilt. Deep down, her mother blamed herself for abiding by her husband's wishes to keep the threat of the cartel from their youngest daughter and the man they'd considered a son.

'If they had told you…would you have told me?' he asked after a long pause. She knew it was her own fertile imagination making his voice sound huskier than normal. Once, she had imagined all sorts of things from the tone of his voice. None of it had been right.

'Yes.'

'Even if they'd asked you not to?'

'Yes.' She had not a doubt in her mind. If she'd had the slightest hint of the danger they had been in, she would have swallowed her pride and called Santi.

The traffic started moving again. Elsa put the car into gear and crawled along with it. 'It was only because you took charge of our security that I felt able to go back to Vienna. I could trust the new security team only because you trusted them.'

On her visits home before her father's death, being in Santi's orbit had always been difficult. Avoiding his gaze, avoiding his company had always left her emotionally drained, and she'd felt it even more deeply in those weeks after her father's murder. But Santi's stepping in to take control of her family's security had given her a peace of mind she'd barely understood. She'd barely understood anything back then, too racked with grief to do more than go through the motions of life.

Why had she listened to her mother and pregnant sister when, ten days after the funeral, they'd insisted she return to Vienna?

Valencia or Vienna, it made little difference. Her life was destroyed wherever she lived. But she hadn't known that then. Her bereavement leave from work had been up and she'd returned to her self-made life not realising the safety of the world she'd blindly, selfishly, trusted to always orbit in her favour had shattered to pieces. *She'd* shattered. She'd become suspicious of everyone. She'd only left her apartment in daylight hours and even then had still seen shadows everywhere.

She'd spent the past year trying her hardest to put the shattered pieces back together. Only in the last month had she felt that she'd finally turned the corner.

They were crawling closer to the cause of the traffic. The number of emergency services vehicles gave an idea of the seriousness of the accident.

'Don't look,' he urged.

The compulsion to reach over and touch him shocked her with its strength, and she tightened her hold on the steering wheel. 'Don't worry,' she said softly. 'I won't. Don't you look either.'

A lump had formed in Santi's throat. It had been

steadily growing throughout their conversation and now felt big enough to choke him.

The call Rosaria had made to him a year ago had come vividly back to him.

He'd known in an instant that something terrible had happened.

When he'd first heard her sobs, in those few moments before she'd found the words to speak, Santi's heart had stopped beating, every part of him frozen to ice with terror that she would say Elsa's name.

There was a coldness on his lap now too, the bottle of water he'd removed from the glove box for Elsa to drink. Glad of something to distract him from the painful memories, he unscrewed the lid. 'You still want water?'

'Yes, please.' She held her hand out for it.

He pressed the bottle into her palm and, as her fingers closed around it, they brushed against his. Hands that had only just stopped tingling from holding hers became electrified. He clenched his jaw tightly to expel the image of the look in her eyes when they'd come within a feather of kissing.

He must not drop his guard like that again, must not do *anything* to encourage this accelerating awareness.

He placed his clenched fists onto his lap and breathed deeply.

They passed the scene of the accident in silence. Both looked straight ahead, neither wanting to look at an accident that would force their minds to conjure the scene when Marco had been killed.

Then the autostrada cleared and Elsa visibly relaxed and sped up.

As the kilometres passed by, Santi began to relax too. He watched her drive, enjoyed the way her pretty hands manipulated the steering wheel...

But that only brought the craving in his blood back to a heated simmer and let loose fantasies of those same hands manipulating parts of *him*. Dragging his attention away from them, he tried to focus on the scenery surrounding them.

A song he liked came on the radio. He started singing along at the same moment Elsa did. There was a brief moment where she turned her head to look at him, their gazes holding through their dark shades for a short beat before she looked back at the road.

He dropped his own gaze and suddenly noticed the skirt of her dress had ridden to mid-thigh. Once he'd noticed it was *all* he noticed, and he became aware of the muscles in that succulent golden thigh tensing whenever she changed gear. It was enough to make his own muscles tense...

He cursed himself. *Stop looking.*

But he could no more stop his eyes from darting glances at her than he could stop his nostrils inhaling her heady scent.

Two hours after Elsa had taken the wheel he could stand it no longer.

'Let's stop at the next services and get coffee,' he said in a sharper tone than intended.

'Okay.'

When they stopped, he would drive the final leg of their journey to Portofino. With the road to concentrate on rather than Elsa, he could put a firm halt to this sick desire that was starting to consume him.

He had to.

When Elsa opened her eyes, night had fallen. Santi, who'd parked at the back of what looked like a busy hotel, was stretching his back and neck. She looked at her watch. In all, they'd been on the road for twelve hours. He must be exhausted.

'Are we there?' she asked, smothering a yawn.

'Yes. We'll sleep on the yacht and set off first thing in the morning.'

It took only minutes to walk to the marina, which was alive with twinkling lights from the yachts and other boats, people strolling, chattering voices and bursts of music. Pulling her suitcase along, she walked in step with Santi as he took the well-lit right-hand path, and peered at the two super-yachts moored in the distance. It was too far and too dark for her to tell which belonged to him. As they walked, people, many dining and drinking on their sundecks, waved and hailed them.

Santi stopped beside a row of mid-sized gleaming yachts that, while obviously luxurious, were only a fraction of the size of his new yacht.

He pulled a set of keys out of his pocket. 'This is the one.'

'This isn't yours,' she said, confused.

His brow creased. 'We aren't using mine.'

'But you said…' Her voice tailed off as she remembered he hadn't actually said they would be sailing on his yacht, only that they would be sailing. She'd assumed.

He must have caught her thinking for he grimaced. 'We need to be inconspicuous, *chiquita*. *The Conchita* can hardly be described as that.'

'No,' she agreed with a sigh and an internal despairing curse. *The Conchita*, named for his mother, was two hundred feet of ostentation, including the obligatory helipad and submarine, and had taken three years to complete. There had been much fanfare in the European yachting community about it. If the cartel knew about Santi's links to her family, which she assumed they did, and if they were smart, which they were, then they would have spotters reporting on *The Conchita*'s movements.

This yacht was, she estimated, no more than seventy feet.

A gangplank had been lowered onto the mooring path. Santi picked up the cases and carried them on board.

Despite the urge to march herself down to the distant super-yachts and beg a lift to Valencia, Elsa made her legs follow Santi.

She stepped into the interior of the main deck. The quality of the materials used to create the living and dining area, U-shaped galley and helm near the bows were undoubtedly expensive; cherry wood panelling and soft leather furnishings made the whole yacht scream luxury. Everything blended together with seamless panache and under any other circumstances she would have been thrilled with it.

'Where did you get this?'

'Felipe organised the charter. I don't know who owns it.'

She hardly dared to ask. 'How many cabins does it have?'

'Two. Both en suite. They adjoin but have private entrances too.' He pointed to steps heading down beside the helm. 'Those stairs lead to the master suite. The stairs behind you go to the second one. They're identical, so take your pick.'

'Where does the crew sleep?'

He didn't look at her while he answered. 'There isn't a crew.'

Her heart stuttered then roared back to life.

The only thing that had kept her going through the long, torturous drive with Santi had been the thought of a huge yacht she could get lost on and the presence of a crew who would act as buffers between them.

Clasping at straws, she said, 'So who'll…?'

'I will.' He grinned. She knew him well enough to know it was forced. 'I've sailed and navigated similar yachts before. Some owners employ a small crew but these are designed for owners to sail themselves. Remember, *chiquita*, we need to blend in. On this yacht, no one will look twice at us. We'll be just another pair of wealthy lovers enjoying a summer break sailing the Mediterranean together.'

Her stomach flipped violently at the casual way he

bandied the word 'lovers,' but somehow she managed to force brightness into her voice. 'That's a shame. I was looking forward to spending a day or two on *The Conchita*…' As she spoke, it came to her that the much smaller proportions must mean comparatively smaller horsepower. She braced herself before asking, 'How long will it take us to get to Valencia?'

'Four or five days.'

The time she'd thought she had left being stuck with Santi had more than doubled in an instant.

She could feign brightness no more. 'I'm going to explore.'

'Go ahead. I need to check in with Felipe then we can order food. Most of the restaurants on the harbour deliver. There should be menus around somewhere.'

'Feel free to order for me. You know what I like.'

She scuttled down the steps at near the bows of the yacht without looking back, hating that he did know what she liked, probably better than anyone else. Santi was the one person in the world she'd always been completely herself with. She'd never needed to put on a front with him, never told any of the white lies she'd liberally told her parents and sister, never had to act confident when she was feeling insecure like with her friends, never felt she had to prove herself in any way to him.

Yanking the wig off, Elsa forced her thoughts away from Santi and the past to take stock of the cabin. It was far more spacious than she'd expected and tastefully decorated. To the left of the king-size bed was a small dining area, to the right a door she suspected opened to create a private balcony. She'd have to wait until they were at sea to find out. There was also a compact dressing table and plenty of storage. The en suite was beautiful, complete with a large walk-in shower with colourful mosaic tiles. Next to the bathroom door stood another door with a sliding lock. She turned the handle and it opened to reveal the second cabin, laid out as a mirror to the first. She closed the adjoining door quickly and locked it.

She couldn't deny that the yacht would be considered huge by any normal person. For an ordinary couple in love, this would be heaven.

Whatever Elsa's confused feelings for Santi were, romantic love no longer had any part of them but the last thing she wanted was to be stuck in these intimate confines for days and days with him. Not when every nerve in her body vibrated just to think his name.

Santi had just finished his call when Elsa reappeared. She'd removed the wig, her dark auburn hair flowing around her shoulders.

He noticed she kept a healthy distance between them as she eyed the phone in his hand. 'Is everything okay?'

'They're putting the final pieces in place. If everything goes to plan, the cartel's takedown should happen within the next forty-eight hours.' While he accepted the need to ensure every aspect of the takedown was planned to the nth degree, the sooner it happened the better. As soon as it was over the pre-planned contingencies to speedily return Elsa to her family would be enacted.

It couldn't happen soon enough for his liking. When the plans had been drawn up, he'd hardly given a thought to the prospect of spending days on end confined on a small yacht with her. Being confined in a car with Elsa had been a thousand times more difficult than he'd anticipated but at least he'd had the road as a distraction. Here, with the most advanced navigational technology available, distractions would be hard to come by.

'My family?' she asked.

'Safe. Did you choose a cabin?'

'Can I have the front one?'

'Sure.'

He picked up her suitcase and carried it down the steps. Only when he'd placed it on the bed did he realise she'd followed him. The spacious cabin reduced in size in an instant. The only thing that didn't appear shrunken was the bed. It was impossible to look at it with Elsa so close to him and not remember that night…

He'd closed his bedroom door and smelt the alcohol in the air before he'd seen her reflection in the full-length mirror. She'd been lying in his bed.

Trying his damnedest to slam the memories shut, he backed out of the cabin. 'I'll leave you to unpack. Dinner should be with us in half an hour. Do you want to eat inside or out?'

He'd turned slowly to face her. Her returning stare had been bold but the movement of her throat had shown her boldness to be a front. Silently, she'd pinched the covers and pulled them off. Beneath them, she'd been naked.

He punched the image away and willed the heat in his loins to cool. It had been a long day. His brain was exhausted, his mental defences weakened.

'Is it safe to eat outside?' she murmured, gaze resting on the floor.

'As long as you put your wig back on.'

Her auburn hair had fanned across his pillow...

She pulled a face.

He cleared his dry throat. 'Does it hurt?'

'No. It's just a little uncomfortable.'

'I'm sorry.'

'Don't be.' She grimaced and shook her head and then those mesmerising green-brown eyes locked onto his. 'Don't apologise for trying to keep me alive.'

His guts clenched but he kept his voice steady. 'So, inside or out?'

'Out.'

'I'll see you on the sundeck.' He closed the cabin door, tilted his head back and expelled the huge breath of air he'd been holding.

CHAPTER SIX

AFTER HIDING IN her cabin for precisely thirty minutes, ostensibly unpacking and changing for dinner into an emerald-green high-neck maxi-dress, Elsa ventured up to the sundeck.

She found it easily enough, climbing the steps she'd passed at the back of the yacht to find a sizeable dining and seating area, a hot tub that could fit a handful of people in it, and Santi, whose back was to her. He turned at the sound of her footsteps and she saw he'd been examining a second cockpit. He could steer the yacht inside or out. In front of that was a section she guessed was for sunbathing.

It cheered her to know there was more room for privacy—Santi avoidance—than she'd first thought. Judging by the way he'd left her cabin as quickly as he'd entered it, she imagined it cheered him too.

The awkwardness that had emanated from him in those few moments he'd been in her cabin had gone. He grinned to acknowledge her and pointed over her shoulder, where a man carrying a large tray approached their yacht. 'Good timing. That's our dinner. Get comfortable. I'll bring it up.'

The dining area had corner seating around a table that could comfortably accommodate eight people. She sat with her back to the harbour path and noted an outdoor grill and food preparation area. Certain no one could see her, she closed her eyes and welcomed the cooling fresh sea breeze on her face.

Her heart sped up when she heard Santi's nearing footsteps and she swallowed hard.

She'd rid herself of her attraction to him before, she reminded herself grimly. She could do it again. And if she couldn't… She would control it. Hopefully kill it. But she'd never let him see it. Never put either of them in the situation where he had to reject her again.

Santi didn't want her. He never had. He would protect her with his life but physically she repulsed him. That near-kiss had been…nothing. Whatever she thought she kept glimpsing in his eyes was a lie her brain had conjured to torment her.

'Dinner is served.' He placed the tray, which had two covered plates and cutlery on it, on the table before opening a cupboard beside the grill. The cupboard was in fact a fully stocked drinks fridge. He selected a bottle of white wine then opened another cupboard and pulled out two wine glasses.

'Just water for me, thanks,' Elsa said.

A thick black brow rose before he shrugged and exchanged one of the glasses for a tall one. From the fridge he removed a bottle of still water and then placed it all on the table. Once settled, he lifted the silver lids to reveal plates artfully arranged with linguine, clams and delicately roasted cherry tomatoes. One mouthful proved this simple dish had a bagful of flavour.

'Sure you don't want any wine?' Santi asked as he poured himself a large glass.

'I don't drink.'

He remembered all the times he'd picked her up from parties the worse for wear and how she'd often commented about looking forward to turning eighteen so her alcohol consumption couldn't be policed any more. He also remembered her parents' bemusement that their party-loving daughter had obtained a first-class degree and been given a special award from the university. The most they'd hoped for was that she would scrape a pass. 'Since when?'

She shrugged and set her gaze on the horizon. 'What are we going to do about food when we're at sea?'

'We're fully stocked with provisions. Since when don't you drink?'

She placed another forkful of linguine into her mouth.

'You're not going to answer?'

She pointed to her full mouth with one hand and twirled linguine onto her fork with the other. 'Why do you want to know?' she countered once she'd swallowed her food.

'It's a simple question requiring a simple answer. I don't understand why you're making it into an issue.'

And he didn't understand why the answer felt so damn important.

'I'm not. I haven't touched alcohol in a long time.'

He watched her put another forkful into her mouth, observed the tightness of her jaw as she chewed, noted the way she looked at everything but him.

'How long? What made you give up?' What would she do if he leaned over the table and ran his tongue over her tight jawline…?

What in hell was he *thinking*?

'This is sounding like the Inquisition again.'

'If this was the Inquisition your red hair would have you burned as a heretic,' he teased, even as his mind once again conjured that flame of hair over his pillow. 'Is a little light conversation too much to ask?'

Light conversation to get them through this meal before he escaped to the privacy of his cabin where he would do his damnedest not to think that only a door separated her from him.

'Not at all. I just don't get why I have to be the one answering everything.'

'Then let's take it in turns. Truthful, non-evasive answers of more than one syllable only. You start. Ask me anything.'

'Okay…' Her mouth made the swirling motion as she thought. 'Why the beard?'

He rubbed his fingers over it. 'When your *mamá* asked me to escort you home, I thought I should disguise myself a little.'

'You grew that in a few days?'

'Five days.'

'Impressive.'

He rubbed it again. 'Must be all the testosterone. Do you like it?'

Why the *hell* had he asked her that?

She shrugged. Did he imagine the tinge of colour on her cheeks? 'If you like beards.'

'Do you like beards?'

He was going to cut his tongue out, he thought grimly. The tongue now tingling as he imagined running it down the arch of her neck...

He straightened his spine and willed the heat in his loins to abate. Mind over matter.

'I've never thought about it.' Not until Santi had grown one and Elsa had found her fingers itching to stroke it and her skin tingling to remember that one brief brush of it against her cheek when he'd met her in Vienna. 'Is your hair slicked back for disguise purposes too?'

'Yes.' He had a large drink of his wine and flashed his teeth. 'My turn.'

She braced herself for a personal question she wouldn't want to answer.

'Can you see yourself moving back to Valencia?'

Relief made her relax and smile. 'One day.'

'Elaborate.'

'I love Vienna but don't see myself living there for ever. I still think of Valencia as home.'

He twirled a large heap of linguine expertly around his fork before it disappeared into his mouth.

Suddenly aware that she was raptly watching him eat, Elsa wrenched her gaze back to her own food.

Frightened that her fingers had as much substance as the linguine and that her heart rate had accelerated again, she hurriedly said, 'My turn. What was the worst thing you did as a teenager?'

His features tightened. His eyes narrowed and visibly darkened.

Having thought he'd laugh and say something along the lines of petty vandalism, she was taken aback at the visceral reaction and put her fork back on her plate. 'What did you do?' she repeated quietly.

A pulse beat loudly in Santi's head. He rubbed the back of his neck and met her stare. 'Have you ever done something that makes your stomach twist and shame hit you like a hot wave whenever you think of it?'

Something flickered over her face. A wince of pain. Colour stained her cheeks. She gave a short, sharp nod.

He grimaced. 'I put my PE teacher in hospital.'

Her eyes widened then blinked. Blinked again. *'Why?'*

He took a large swig of his wine before reaching for the bottle to top his glass up. 'Because I lost control.'

Elsa stared at him. '*You* lost control?' The Santi she knew was always in control. Always. The only times he'd lost his cool around her had been that fateful night and when he'd threatened to shove her in the boot of the car. Both times, she admitted painfully, she'd deserved his temper.

He pushed his plate to one side. 'My mother's death...

Look, I'm not going to make excuses but her death ripped me in two. I couldn't handle it. The pain. That's when I started acting out. If not for your father I would have been expelled for any number of reasons. Fighting. Stealing. Truanting, and Mr Perez hated me for that. He was a sadistic bully at the best of times, but the thing he really despised me for was setting fire to his personal fiefdom: the school gym.'

'You *didn't*?' she breathed, partly in awe. Elsa had hardly been considered a good girl at school but her bad behaviour had been more mischievous than actually bad.

His eyes glinted. 'I set a firework off in it. Don't worry—it was empty. No one got hurt. Your father paid for the repairs and gave a hefty donation to the school in exchange for me getting away with a short suspension.'

'Is that what caused the fight?' she asked, agog. She hadn't known *any* of this.

He grimaced. 'A fight means two or more people hitting each other. This was no fight.'

'So what happened?'

'My last day of school. I left thinking I would never return but I'd forgotten to clear my locker out. It had a pair of trainers your parents bought me for my birthday in it, so I went back. I got my trainers but when I went back outside, Mr Perez was walking to his car. The place was deserted. As soon as he saw me he squared up to me. Shouted abuse. Taunted me. Told me I didn't deserve your family. That I was a nasty piece of shit. All the things he'd spent three years wanting to say.'

His features tensed immeasurably. 'Something in me snapped. I dragged him behind his car and beat the hell out of him. Knocked him out cold. Broke his jaw and nose and fractured an eye socket.'

Elsa had always known her giant protector was more than capable of looking after himself but, even though he'd already said he'd put the teacher in hospital, the details still made her wince with horror. 'Oh, Santi, *no*,' she whispered. What a thing for him to have to live with.

He pinched the bridge of his nose and jerked a grim nod.

'Were you arrested?'

'Not that time.'

Her brows drew together in confusion.

'I'd been arrested twice before that. Your father bailed me out both times. This time I panicked. I called an ambulance and ran home. Confessed everything to your father—he knew the issues I'd had with Mr Perez. I wanted to hand myself in but he asked me to wait a day.'

'Ah…' She sighed, understanding. 'He paid him off?'

He gave a grim nod. 'A million euros for his silence.'

Her jaw dropped. Even for her father, that was a staggering act of generosity. Or desperation. The latter, she decided. Her father had loved Santi like a son.

'Your father pointed out to Perez that I had no money of my own. I could go to prison and he would receive nothing or he could take the money that would set him up for life. He chose greed over justice.' The ghost of a smile played on his lips. 'He quit teaching and moved to Thailand. He even sent me a postcard.'

Her chest loosened. 'He wasn't too traumatised then?'

'If he was, he hid it well. He always was a hard nut but I shouldn't have let him provoke me. I was eighteen. An adult. Your father had done everything to get me back on the straight and narrow, and while he paid Mr Perez off and hushed everything up, he made it clear it was my last chance. That, and the guilt I felt, was the wake-up call I needed to turn my life around.'

'Did he read you the riot act?' she asked, feeling a pang of melancholy.

'Yes. He did it in that quiet way he had. You remember?'

'He didn't have to raise his voice, did he?' she whispered.

'He never raised his voice.'

'That was always the worst. I used to wish he would shout at me like Mamá did.' Elsa often looked back and wondered why she'd ever felt it necessary to lie to someone so enduringly kind and non-judgemental.

Those bastards who'd killed her father had extinguished a candle of light in this dark world. She wished she could be there to witness their downfall. She prayed it involved excruciating pain.

'Does it make you think differently about me?' he asked, eyes locking back on hers.

She shook her head. 'Maybe it would have done before Papá died but not now. You lost your mother so young… Sometimes there is no rhyme or reason to how we react to grief.'

Growing up, Elsa had assumed everyone had the same happy life she'd enjoyed. She remembered feeling intensely sorry for Santi when his mother died because he didn't have a *mamá* any more, but at only four she'd been far too young to understand the finality of death and the grief that could tear a bereaved person's soul in two. She'd only truly understood that a year ago. She couldn't imagine how it would be to lose a parent you loved when you were only fifteen and full of combustible hormones.

Frightened by how badly she wanted to wrap her arms around him, and feeling a strong need to lighten the heavy mood, she said, 'I hope Papá made the teacher sign something that stopped him coming back for more money. If he hears how much you're worth now, he'll kick himself for selling out too cheap.'

She was rewarded with a rumble of laughter that dived straight into her bloodstream and heated her unbearably. 'It was water-tight.'

'Good…' She wanted to add something but hesitated.

Santi noticed. 'What?'

She sighed.

'When have you ever not been able to say what's on your mind to me?' he asked gently.

Her smile contained such sadness that for a moment he thought his heart had splintered. The tips of her fingers extended to touch his, just a light brush of skin against skin but enough to make his blood tingle.

'I was just thinking of how proud Papá was of you. And now I know why. You really did turn your life around.'

His brain told his hand to move. His hand disobeyed.

'All thanks to him,' he said heavily.

Her throat moved. Something glimmered in her eyes. 'I think you might have had a little involvement too,' she rebuked softly, threading her fingers between his…or was it him threading his fingers through hers?

Darts of desire unleashed and fired through him, and he finally got control of his hand and pulled it away, but it was too late. The spread was relentless. He clenched his teeth together and fisted his hands but still awareness flickered in every part of him, and suddenly he knew that when it came to Elsa, mind over matter was impossible. His desire for her had infected him. Every minute spent together had seen it burrow deeper under his skin, and when she looked at him the way she was looking now, as if she was trapped in his stare and helpless to pull out of it, the infection burned through his barriers.

He would not let it burn any closer.

With huge effort, he un-fisted his hands and placed them heavily on the table, then leaned forward so she could not mistake a single word he said. 'After the incident with Mr Perez, your father kept me close. Gave me a role in his business. He put his faith in me and taught me everything I needed to be a man. Do you understand that? I cannot state this enough—everything I am and everything I have is down to him, and I would *never* betray him.'

Her eyes widened slightly. Her chest rose.

Listen to me! he wanted to shout. *Understand. Keep your distance. For both our sakes.*

It felt as if for ever passed before her eyes flickered and her lips formed into a taut smile. She got to her feet, her movements far jerkier than her usual elegance, but her voice was clear and light when she spoke. 'I know what my father meant to you and what you meant to him but you can't give him all the credit for what you've achieved. That was down entirely to your own hard work.

'Now, I hope you don't mind, but I'm going to bed. I'm exhausted. Thank you for dinner. Sleep well.'

Santi watched her silhouette disappear down the stairs with a heart so tightly clenched that any relief was nullified.

Twenty minutes later and Santi hadn't moved. He didn't dare. The longing to follow Elsa into her cabin was just too strong.

He put his face in his hands and kneaded his fingers into his skin.

This was impossible. His desire for her. It could never be.

Their conversation had taken an unanticipated route. Her horror had been apparent but so too had her empathy. He didn't know why the latter should shock him, not when she had Marco's and Rosaria's blood in her.

That was the first time he'd spoken of the incident with the teacher since it had happened. From that day on, he'd had two goals in life—to repay Marco's faith and make him and Rosaria proud.

Any pride he'd earned would be stripped away if they could read his thoughts and see the depth of his torturous desire for their daughter. It was the main thing that had stopped him acting on it that night five years ago, and nausea swelled inside him as the doors he'd slammed on the memories swung on their hinges and that night replayed itself to him in full, vivid Technicolor for the first time.

He'd arrived home to his cottage late and badly out of sorts. He'd carried the image of Elsa's naked silhouette with him all that day. He didn't imagine how he could feel worse about himself.

And then he'd found her in his bed.

He could still remember the exact way his heart had thumped. The way his stomach had dropped. The way his throat had run dry. The fire that had burned his blood.

Without a word, she'd pinched the bedsheets and slowly pulled them off her.

The body he'd spent the day trying to banish from his memory had revealed itself in its full glory. The fire in his blood had become a furnace, heating his skin as his violently beating heart had pumped it relentlessly through him.

Dear sweet Lord. She had been perfect.

Creamy golden skin, plump high breasts topped with

dark rose nipples, a slender waist, a pubis with a light triangle of hair a shade darker than that on her head, perfectly rounded thighs, lithe golden legs…

'Are you not going to join me?' she'd asked.

Later, he was to think gratefully that if those seductive words hadn't been delivered with a slur, he would have succumbed to her wanton invitation. Dear God, he was only human.

He'd grabbed the back of his neck and breathed in deeply, trying to get control of himself. He'd felt like *he* was drunk and had stumbled into the sweetest nightmare possible.

'Santi?' She'd propped herself up a little. Her breasts had moved tantalisingly.

He'd screwed his eyes shut. 'You shouldn't be here. You need to leave.'

'You don't mean that.' She'd hiccupped. And then she'd laid her head back and spread her arms wide. Welcoming him. Inviting him. 'Make love to me, Santi.'

Something inside him had snapped and he had suddenly been filled with utter self-loathing and, at that moment, hatred for Elsa too for putting him in that position.

'You're drunk,' he'd said, still trying to keep a lid on the temper now rising with as much passion as his longing.

'I know.' She'd hiccupped again.

'Go home, Elsa. I'll leave you to put your clothes on.' Determined not to look at her, he'd walked to the door but her reflexes had worked much better than he'd have thought considering her state of inebriation. Giggling, she'd thrown herself across the bed and grabbed hold of his arm before he could escape.

'Don't be like this, Santi.' Her words had become so slurred they'd been barely recognisable. 'I *love* you. I've been waiting for you *for ever*. And you love me. We're going to get married and…'

He'd shaken her off his arm as if she were a terrier biting into his skin. 'What the *hell* are you playing at?' he'd snarled. 'Do you have any idea what a dangerous game this is? You break into my home and wait in my bed for me like a common slut? You were raised better than this. You should be ashamed of yourself.'

Her eyes had widened and she'd shuffled unsteadily back, shaking her head as if he'd suddenly sprouted a second head. Her voice became very small. 'Don't you want me?'

'*No*!' he'd roared, as much to himself as to her. 'You're my mentor's daughter!' He'd needed to get away, out of the cottage and off the Lopez estate before he did something he regretted. Like haul her into his arms and take every ounce of pleasure she had been offering.

But only animals took advantage of drunken women and he was not an animal. And only disloyal bastards betrayed those who'd saved them and given them everything by bedding their virgin daughter, and he would sooner cut his hands off than betray Marco.

Damn Elsa. Damn her for putting him in this position. Damn her for betraying their friendship. And damn her for turning his blood to liquid and his loins to fire in the blink of an eye.

Her chin had wobbled, eyes filling with tears. 'Is that all you see me as?'

'Yes, it is.' The knowledge he'd spent the day doing his utmost not to imagine himself making love to her had only fuelled his fury.

Her clothes had been in a pile by the side of the bed. On the top of it had been a lacy red bra.

His self-loathing had ratcheted to self-combust level. He'd picked the pile up and thrown it at her. 'Cover yourself up. Next time you want to lose your virginity, do it with someone who actually wants it and preferably your own age.'

And then he'd walked out of the room, slamming the door behind him, not knowing those would be the last words he spoke to her for five years.

CHAPTER SEVEN

Movement overhead woke Elsa from the light sleep she'd finally fallen into. She shuffled to the edge of the bed and peered through the blinds. All she could see was the deep blue of the surrounding sea and the azure of the bright cloudless sky. Santi had set sail.

Just to think his name was to set her heart racing. To remember how their fingers had laced together, the feelings that had erupted through her...

She put a hand to her chest and breathed deeply, told herself to get a grip and then propelled herself to the en suite.

The touch of their fingers... What had she been *thinking*? It had happened without any conscious thought on her part. She could only assume that their conversation, what he'd confessed, the way he'd opened up to her... The impulse to touch him had been beyond her control.

And then he'd yanked his hand away as if her touch had scalded him. Had he been able to read her mind? Had he known the effect that small touch had had on her? Was that the reason he'd felt it necessary to put her back in her place with the reminder that she was his mentor's daughter and nothing more?

She stepped under the shower and vowed not to dissect the evening again. She'd spent enough time doing that during her mostly sleepless night spent fidgeting and pacing and doing her very best not to look at the door separating their cabins.

After she'd dressed, she made her bed and just…hovered. She might have hovered for hours if her stomach hadn't rumbled.

She kneaded her forehead. She couldn't hide away like a frightened squirrel and starve just because *she* was the one having a problem with her self-control. Santi was there for one reason only and that was her safety. He'd disrupted his life to protect her. It wasn't his fault she responded to him so physically. It never had been.

Squaring her shoulders, telling herself that she could do this, could act like everything was fine, she left the cabin.

She found him on the main deck. He was sat at the helm, studying the screens surrounding it. All he wore was a pair of tan shorts, a sight that immediately made her belly turn to mush and her resolve to act normally was almost scuppered from her first look as her greedy eyes absorbed his hard muscularity.

He lifted his head to greet her. 'Good morning, *chiquita*. Did you sleep well?'

She dragged her eyes from his chest to his face but

there was no relief to be found there, not when her heart sighed with joy to meet the glittering black eyes.

She forced her lips into a smile and was thankful she could speak coherently. 'It took a while but I got there.' A while being a good eight hours of wakefulness compared to probably three hours of actual sleep. 'How long have you been up?'

'Hours. I wanted to set sail before the marina woke up.'

'Have you eaten?' she asked politely.

'Hours ago. If you look through the cupboards you'll find breakfast stuff. Don't worry about running low, there's extra supplies below deck.'

She wandered to the galley. Although small, it had ample storage, the cupboards filled with provisions. The tall fridge was crammed with fresh goods and from it she pulled out a pot of yogurt then took a banana from the fruit bowl.

'Do you want anything?' How hard it was to keep her voice even. How much harder to keep her eyes to herself. She couldn't stop them darting to him or help the throb of heat low in her abdomen to see the smoothness of his bronzed back and the way the muscles bunched as he went about his business at the helm.

'I could murder a coffee if you don't mind making it?'

'Of course not,' she answered airily, relieved that when she set her mind to it, she could act so...*normal*. That was the key to getting through the next few days, she decided. To mask all the heated feelings consuming her and act normal.

While Elsa busied herself in the kitchen, Santi concentrated on the job in hand. It had been a while since he'd last been at the helm of a yacht and he wanted to have total confidence that he'd done everything correctly in setting their course before he turned the autopilot on. He'd been immersed in it and now found himself having to concentrate hard to get his head back in the zone and tune out Elsa's presence as she swished around in her pretty knee-length caftan.

It had been many years since he'd had such a bad night's sleep and he knew it was reliving the locked memories that had caused it. For five years he'd tried his damnedest to block that night from his brain. He'd refused to allow his mind to travel there. Elsa's move to Vienna had freed him. In truth, he'd been relieved. No more crippling guilt for desiring his mentor and saviour's daughter.

But the image of Elsa in his bed had sneaked up on him in those times when he was tired. He would bat it away but the image would linger.

Forgetting that night had been hard. Forgetting Elsa had been impossible. Now that the memories had been unlocked, the desire he'd been battling had accelerated in its intensity.

Shame on him but he'd found his ear pressed to the adjoining door to her cabin, his heart thudding as he'd listened to her movements before he'd come to his senses and hastily moved away.

He'd lain on his bed with the air-conditioning set to arctic and tried to think of anything but Elsa.

It had proved impossible. Everything about Elsa was proving impossible.

'Do you need my help with anything?' she asked, interrupting his moody thoughts. She held his coffee out.

He removed the cup carefully, making sure their fingers didn't touch. 'No. I'm good, thanks.'

She smiled and stepped back. 'I'm going to my cabin. Shout if you need me.'

'Will do,' he lied. If he had his way, she could stay in her cabin until this whole nightmare was over.

After spending the day sunbathing on her private balcony—she had been right, the door in her cabin did open to create one—Elsa had run out of bottled water. With great reluctance, she ventured out to the main deck for only the second time since breakfast. The first time, when she'd come out for some lunch, she'd quickly chopped herself a hunk of French bread, grabbed a handful of grapes and scarpered back to her cabin without seeing him. She wasn't so fortunate this time. He was sitting at the dining table, chatting on his phone. His olive skin seemed to have turned three shades darker since breakfast.

Avoiding direct contact with his eyes, she hurried past him. Her hands trembled as she raided the fridge, blood pounding in her head, but she forced her spine to stay straight and tried with all her might to tune out the sound of his voice.

She was just about to walk back to her cabin when his call finished.

'That was Felipe,' he informed her.

Apprehension building, she swallowed before looking at him, still avoiding direct eye contact.

'It appears the cartel has fallen for the decoy.'

She didn't have the faintest idea what he was talking about.

'When we set sail this morning, a crew of ex-special forces set sail on *The Conchita* from Genoa. There are three suspicious yachts keeping distant pace with it.'

'The cartel think we're on your yacht?'

'When you and I left Vienna, a redheaded lady of approximately your age and size and a dark-haired man of approximately my age and size were spotted fleeing the city by a different route. They arrived in Genoa last night and boarded *The Conchita*. They set sail this morning at around the same time we left Portofino, taking a different route to ours.'

She was too desperate to escape to give more than a fleeting acknowledgement to the cleverness of the plan. 'That's brilliant,' she said, inching closer to the steps back to her cabin. 'Where are we sailing to?'

'First stop Corsica. There's an excellent bay we can anchor in tonight—it's safer to avoid the marina. I don't want to take any chances.'

Why did the mention of night set butterflies loose in her belly?

'We should arrive within the hour,' he continued.

'I'll rustle up something for dinner when we're safely anchored.'

'Okay. Thank you. See you in a few hours.' But in her haste to escape, she caught her arm on the seat of the helm and dropped the bottles she was carrying.

Cheeks flaming, she crouched down to pick them up. One of the bottles had rolled and landed at Santi's giant foot. Everything then happened very quickly. She extended an arm to it but at the exact moment her fingers wrapped around it he leaned down for it too and his fingers wrapped around hers.

Their eyes clashed before she could stop it happening.

A breathless moment passed.

A pulse shot out of the blackness of his eyes. A depth that made her feel stripped to the bone and filled with such longing that, suddenly, she couldn't breathe. Heat flowed through her veins as if an electric current had been set off inside her, melting her like ice cream.

The connection was severed abruptly when Santi jerked his head and let go of her hand. 'I need to be on the sundeck,' he said tightly, before straightening and heading outside.

He didn't look back.

How desperately could a man crave a woman? And how deep could the craving run before madness set in?

Those were the questions plaguing Santi as he tried to force his brain to engage with the navigation systems. It felt like he'd had some form of kinetic energy injected into his veins.

Never in his life had he wanted a woman the way he wanted Elsa.

Damn it, he wasn't made of stone. He was a flesh and blood man and she was the woman his flesh and blood sang for. One look was enough for his body to come to life.

As hard as he fought it, something was happening between them. It had started when their gazes had caught in the Viennese courtyard, a nebulous chemical reaction swirling around them, pulling them closer together, a powerful force of nature it was growing almost impossible to push back against.

Why did it have to be *her*?

And why was his heart already thrumming with anticipation for what the rest of their time at sea would bring when he knew it would not bring anything?

He wouldn't, *couldn't*, allow it.

Elsa locked her door and tried her hardest to catch her breath. For a few, heady moments she'd stared into Santi's eyes and thought she'd seen...

What?

Desire? Real emotions?

Fool.

The beats of her heart wouldn't settle.

She had to fight this. She'd deluded herself once about Santi. She'd allowed herself to believe her feelings for him were reciprocated because that's what she'd *wanted* to believe. She'd read things that simply weren't there. The one time when she'd really felt something from him, that electric connection the morning after her eighteenth birthday party, had proved itself to be the biggest delusion of all.

Never again would she put herself in the position of waking cold and ashamed with the memories of Santi's cruel rejection ringing in her ears before she'd even opened her eyes. She would not read things that weren't there. She would not allow herself to be torn apart by her own imagination again.

She was not that girl any more.

The sun was setting magnificently, an orange haze on the horizon, the first stars winking their presence in the darkening skies. Santi, staring at the distant Corsican landscape, bottle of beer in hand, didn't think there had existed a more perfect, romantic setting.

Romantic?

Where in the bowels of hell had that thought come from? Until that exact minute Santi had never had a romantic thought in his life. Romance was for women, and for the unscrupulous men who wanted to bed them by taking the easy route. The only flowers Santi had ever bought were yellow roses for his mother's grave. He'd been in exactly one jewellery shop and that had been to purchase the watch on his wrist.

Faint footsteps echoed below. He turned his head and held his breath. A moment later, Elsa joined him on the sundeck.

The sensation of his lungs slowly collapsing filled him and he reflexively tightened his hold on the rail.

Like him, Elsa had showered and dressed for dinner, a habit as natural for her as breathing but one he'd adopted through all the meals he'd shared with the Lopezes.

All his good manners came from observing and copying the Lopezes', from not bolting his food, to opening doors for ladies, to speaking respectfully to his elders. His mother had been a diamond in the rough, born in a bad neighbourhood and raised with kids for whom school had been a dirty word. While she'd taken pride in sending Santi to school every day in immaculately clean and pressed clothes, it would never have crossed her mind that her son eating with his mouth open would be considered rude.

For all the trappings of his wealth, Santi was still that poor, rough, ill-mannered boy.

Elsa's good breeding was an innate part of her. Everything, from the way she ate to the way she sat, was graceful. Even when she'd drunk a little more than was good for her she'd been inebriated with style.

He'd only seen her properly drunk that night in his bedroom.

Tonight, she wore a high-necked sleeveless rust-coloured dress with tiny buttons running from the neck that fell to her ankles and tied at the waist. To complement it, she'd donned a pair of gold-heeled sandals that gave her a couple of inches of extra height, applied a little make-up and added a pair of gold hooped earrings.

She could only look more beautiful if her natural red hair was flowing around her shoulders rather than the much shorter dark brown wig she was forced to wear. There were too many other vessels anchored in the bay for them to risk her not wearing it.

He had another drink to settle his careering pulses before saying evenly, 'You look nice.'

'Thank you.' Elsa felt her cheeks flame and looked down at her feet before her eyes were drawn back to him. 'Your hair's gone curly,' she murmured unthinkingly, and clenched her hands into fists to stop them reaching out to touch it. She'd always wanted to touch it.

His lips curved. 'You prefer it curly?'

She nodded. 'It's more…you.' The black shirt he wore with charcoal trousers was more him too. He'd buttoned it to just below his throat. The gold chain around his neck glinted.

His chest rose as he inhaled deeply. That look in his eyes…

She couldn't tear her gaze from the black depths, swirling and ringing with…

Not with what she was looking for, she scolded herself quickly and firmly, pulling herself out of the spell she'd been in danger of falling into. That was *not* a look of desire in his eyes.

She found a smile and said, 'Something smells good.'

He blinked. If she didn't know better she would think he'd been pulled under a spell too. 'That will be the red snapper on the barbecue.'

'How old is it?' she asked doubtfully. She only liked

fish if she could taste the sea in it and they hadn't been near a fishmonger in four days.

'About three hours.' His face broke into a wide grin that made the lines around his eyes crease and her heart sing. 'Caught by my own fair hands. Please, take a seat. Our appetisers are served.'

She pinched the skirt of her dress and sat, admiring the spread he'd laid out for them: slices of salami and prosciutto, tomato and basil bruschetta, olives and breadsticks.

And then she sighed.

What a perfect setting for a romantic meal.

Dusky though the skies were, Corsica's beauty still dazzled. The marina in the distance was packed with yachts of all sizes, overlooked by a citadel and surrounded by mountains.

Yes. The most perfect romantic setting.

But not for them. Never for them.

She filled her glass with iced water from the jug and helped herself to the appetisers, all the while chanting the mantra 'Act normal, act normal,' as she'd prepared herself before leaving the cabin.

'Have you spoken to your family today?' he asked after they'd eaten a few bites.

Relieved at having something neutral to talk about, she told him, 'I had a chat with Marisa earlier. She's determined that whatever happens, the engagement party will go ahead... Have you met her fiancé?'

He gave a dismissive snort. 'He's a wimp.'

Elsa couldn't help her bark of laughter.

He held his hands up defensively. 'I don't understand what she sees in him.'

'He knows the shipping industry inside out so can help her run the business—you know Mamá wants to retire,' she explained. 'He's too rich to be a gold-digger, and Nikos needs a father.'

He pulled a face. 'I agree he needs a father but when you compare his real father to that wet biscuit...'

'His real father's dead.' Nikos Manolas had died in a tragic yachting accident eighteen months ago. His body had never been found.

It suddenly occurred to her that the tragedy should have made her wary of stepping on a similar vessel. It should have made her mother and sister wary too. Elsa knew as well as she knew her own name that they'd swallowed their concerns for the same reason she'd not had any. Because of Santi.

To Elsa and her family, his name was synonymous with safety.

If only she could say the same for her heart.

'I know.' Santi's voice brought her back to the present. 'I knew him well.'

'Were you friends?'

'As much as anyone could be friends with him.' His eyes narrowed. 'You know Marisa's fiancé has a lover?'

'Marisa knows it too. She doesn't care. She doesn't love him. She just wants protection and security for the business and a father for her baby.'

His eye were scrutinising. 'You think she's making a mistake?'

'It's not for me to judge. I'm not in her shoes.'

His expression changed in an instant, a rumble of laughter escaping his throat. 'You can't have changed that much! You used to have an opinion on everything.'

Remembering how he'd always humoured her ill-informed opinions, she poked her tongue out at him before she even realised she was doing it, but the giggles about to escape her lips faded before they could form.

Sharing food, sharing laughter, sharing memories…

These were things that filled her with so much emotion it hurt to look at him.

'Go on,' he urged. 'Your real opinion on your sister's engagement.'

'I'll tell you my opinion if you promise to keep it to yourself.'

Promise not to…

Promise to…

'I promise.'

Leaning forward so she could hug her constricting belly and trying desperately hard not to let him see how this rework of so many long-ago conversations was affecting her, she said, 'Okay, if you really want my opinion…'

'I do,' he assured her.

She took a deep breath. 'I think she's making the biggest mistake of her life. How either of them think they can create a marriage when there's no feeling between them is beyond me, and how Marisa can expect him to grow feelings for baby Nikos when it's obvious Raul only has feelings for himself is beyond me too. But there's no talking to her. Nikos's death almost destroyed her. Marrying Raul is the safe option. She doesn't love him so there's no chance of him hurting her, and while I think she's wrong, I understand completely why she's doing it. When your heart's been broken you do everything you can to protect it from ever happening again.'

Elsa knew immediately that she'd said the wrong thing. It was there in the sudden stillness of Santi's huge frame and the penetration of his stare.

After long, tense moments, he quietly said, 'Who hurt you?'

CHAPTER EIGHT

ANGUISH ROSE FROM deep inside her. How badly Elsa regretted her past openness with Santi. All her hopes and fears, her dreams, all the trials of her life; the fallings-out with friends, the screaming arguments with her mother, the fights with her sister…she'd shared everything. As a result, he could read her like a book.

She fought to keep her poise, reminding herself that he *used* to be able to read her like a book. 'I was talking hypothetically.'

His eyes narrowed and he drained the last of his beer before getting to his feet and taking the three steps to the inbuilt barbecue. He lifted the lid, releasing a wonderful lemony aroma. 'Are you sure? Because if someone's hurt you, I want to know about it.' He used tongs to remove the foil-wrapped fish and place them on a plate. 'Was it Stefan?' he added casually.

She shook her head, tearing her gaze from him and fixing it on the yacht closest to them. 'Looks like they're having a party,' she said, somehow managing to speak through a throat choked with emotion. Music was playing and there had to be a couple of dozen people on the deck.

'Why don't you want to talk about him? What did he do to you?'

'Nothing.'

'Look me in the eye and tell me he did nothing to you.'

Laughter from the partying yacht carried in the air. A pang of envy ripped through her. Elsa had forgotten how much she'd loved to party. She'd loved dressing up and dancing and gossiping and trying concoctions created from whatever she and her friends had been able to pilfer from their parents' alcohol cabinets.

'Elsa.' There was a warning tone in Santi's voice that pierced the beats thudding painfully in her head.

Her gaze flew to him. He stood beside the grill facing her with his arms folded across his powerful chest, black eyes glittering with something that made her belly dive and swoop in one seamless motion.

'Stefan's married,' she blurted out.

The shock on his face would have been comical if her heart hadn't been shredding. 'You had an affair with a married man?'

'There was no affair. He's my boss.'

So many emotions flickered over his face that it was impossible to pick out only one. He blew out a long breath and rubbed the back of his neck. 'Explain.'

She shrugged helplessly. 'I lied.'

And lies always caught up with you. It was a lesson every child learned.

'*Why?*'

'To stop them worrying. Mamá latched on to Stefan's name when I told her about work. I let her believe we were a couple only because I knew how much she wanted me to meet someone.'

'And the other men you said you'd dated? Were they lies too?'

'Not all of them.' She'd accepted the occasional date over the years. Desperation to rid her head of Santi had driven her to accepting them but they'd been fool's errands.

'Were you serious about any of them?'

'No.' Her admission came out as a whisper.

'Were your tales of partying lies too?'

'Yes.'

'Have you drunk alcohol at all since moving to Vienna?'

Her features tightened, lips clamping together, but she shook her head in answer.

'What did you spend your student years doing, then?'

'Studying.'

Studying? Elsa? The girl who'd had screaming matches with her mother over her refusal to do homework, the girl with such a zest for life and adventure, had spent her student years *studying*?

'*Why, chiquita*? Why all the lies?'

'To stop them worrying.'

His laughter had a sarcastic tinge to it. 'You let your family think you were drinking and partying too much to stop them worrying? How the hell does that work?'

'Because they would have thought there was something wrong.'

'But there *was* something wrong.' Santi knew it in his guts. He'd known it since he'd detected that first lie at the beginning of their road trip. 'What happened to you, Elsa? Someone hurt you.'

'Santi, will you please drop it? Let the past stay in the past.' The plea was in her voice as well as her words but he ignored it, too close to unravelling the mysteries that were driving him insane to be deterred any longer.

'Not until you tell me why you went from a fun-loving young woman to a recluse.'

Her shoulders hunched as she bunched her hands together on her lap. 'I didn't turn into a recluse. I changed, that's all. People do change, you of all people should know that.'

'I've learned to control the worst of my instincts but I haven't changed. I'm still the same person underneath.' Still the same poor, rough, ill-mannered boy but in bespoke tailored clothes.

'And I've learned to control my instincts too.' Her eyes flashed. She spoke with an air of triumph, as if she'd found an excuse to latch on to. 'I stopped abusing alcohol…'

'You abused it no more than your average teenager.' Other than that final night.

'I moved to Vienna for a fresh start. I always intended to take university seriously.'

'I don't believe you,' he said flatly.

'I don't care if you believe me.'

He picked up the bowl with the accompaniment he'd made for their fish and slammed it on the table. 'I think you're lying through your pretty little teeth.'

She flinched. 'Don't say that.'

'Then stop lying,' he snarled, leaning down so his face was directly before her. 'Do you forget I have known you since you were a bump in your mother's stomach? I've watched you tell your parents a hundred lies. I hear it in your voice. I know all your little tells. Look at your fingers—they're rubbing together like they always do when you're spouting your bull.'

Something flickered on her face. She looked down at her hands then back to him. Colour saturated her cheeks then, in one quick, fluid motion, she shoved her chair back, placed her hands flat on the table and leaned forward so it was her face directly before his. 'My bull? *My* bull?'

Her angry breaths feathered against his lips. Her green-brown stare knifed through his chest.

'Why do you need me to spell it out for you?' she said scathingly. 'Have you been so deprived of a woman telling you how wonderful you are these past few days that you'd make me dredge up everything I've spent the past five years trying to forget just to boost your fat ego?'

Santi found himself frozen. The thuds from his heart rose up to join the white noise filling the space between his ears, drowning out everything, even the noise of revelry from the nearby yacht.

'You're an intelligent man, Santi, so stop insulting us both by pretending you don't know who hurt me when all you have to do…' Her voice caught. Her eyes closed, features softening. Her body swayed. And then her eyes flew open and she backed away to the steps with a whispered, 'All you have to do is look in a mirror.'

Elsa fell onto her bed clutching her chest and trying frantically to get air into her lungs.

Days and days of putting on a face and fighting feelings that ballooned by the hour… It was too much. She was exhausted. Tired of pretending. Tired of fighting her turbulent feelings.

But there was no time for her to find any kind of composure for the door opened.

An unbidden wail flew from her mouth and she covered her face before Santi's shape could take form.

'Leave me alone,' she said in a voice that sounded excruciatingly like a whimper.

There was no verbal response and neither did she hear his footsteps walk away or the door close.

'Please, just leave me alone,' she begged. 'I'm sorry for lashing out but I can't do this any more. I can't pretend that spending all this time with you isn't tearing me apart.'

There was a pause. *'Chiquita…'*

'Don't say anything,' she pleaded. 'Please, just let things—'

But her words were cut off when her hands were pulled away and Santi's face was right there, hovering only inches from hers, the black eyes boring into her.

Crouched before her, he was breathing heavily, the

strong nostrils flaring, the sensual lips pulled into a tight line.

Suddenly she couldn't breathe. She could hear nothing but her pulse drumming like a tattoo inside her ears. The world went off kilter and began to spin.

Sensation wafted over her neck as a large hand burrowed into her wig and carefully pulled it off.

Trembling, she closed her eyes, felt his fingers skim over her hair and remove the clip keeping it in place then drag through the tresses. Her trembles grew more violent when he cupped his palm to the back of her head and she felt herself being gently pulled forward. The skin on her face tingled as it sensed him inching closer and closer until the firm lips she'd spent so many years dreaming about pressed against hers.

She couldn't move. Her senses were on overload. The scent of Santi's skin, the warmth of his mouth, the heat of his breath, his touch…

An arm slipped around her waist. The tips of her breasts brushed then flattened against his hard chest. Her pelvis throbbed. His lips moved against hers. Heat suffused her. Her heart thumped so hard the beats echoed all the way to her toes.

He doesn't mean it.

His mouth moved again, lips parting. Her own lips parted with the motion. Her tastebuds sparked to life as a brand-new taste filled her. Santi. His tongue slid into her mouth…

He doesn't mean it.

Her shaking hand found his neck and crept up to

the curly hair she'd spent so many years dreaming of touching. The texture was softer than she'd imagined. She splayed her fingers deeper into it, kneading into his skull as he deepened the kiss and tightened his hold around her. Tiny embers of sensation fired through her from low in her abdomen, growing and pulsing as the desire Santi ignited in her bloomed into a furnace.

He doesn't mean it!

The voice echoing with increasing panic in her head finally penetrated and sanity crashed through her.

Wrenching her face from his, she pushed hard against his chest. *'Don't!'*

Elsa's abrupt rejection almost knocked Santi onto his back.

Heaving himself to his feet, he rubbed the nape of his neck and tried to focus through the pain of his arousal. His skin was scorched from Elsa's touch. Flames licked him. Every part of him.

What was he even doing in her cabin?

Why had he followed her?

His legs had paced behind her before his brain could stop him. His only justification had been to ask her what the hell she'd meant about him having to look in the mirror.

But he knew what she'd meant. God help him. A part of him had known all along.

That night...

It *had* haunted her. As much as it had haunted him. The only man who'd hurt her had been him.

'I'm sorry,' he said hoarsely, backing himself against

the adjoining door. His lungs had stopped working properly, the violent thrashing of his heart paralysing the rest of him. 'I shouldn't have done that.'

'Why did you?' she whispered, raising her ashen face to his.

Because he couldn't not. Because one minute he'd been staring into her beautiful eyes and the next he'd lost himself.

'Was it a punishment?' She must have read the cluelessness on his face for her face contorted. 'I know you don't feel like *that* for me, Santi.' Her head dropped and she clutched tightly at her hair. 'Get out and leave me alone.'

He took a deep breath. He was struggling to think coherently.

'What you said…' He swallowed another constriction in his throat. '… About looking in a mirror. I—'

'I said *get out*!' she interrupted with a scream, jumping to her feet, and before he had the chance to realise what she was doing she'd rushed at him, her fists beating at his chest with a desperation that made his heart ache. 'Don't you think you've done enough damage? Leave me *alone*!'

Grabbing at her flailing hands, he pinned them to her sides. Elsa would never hurt him or anyone intentionally but at that moment she was like a woman possessed.

'How can you be so cruel?' she cried. 'To kiss me like you mean it when we both know I disgust you—'

'What…?' Disgust? Was she crazy? 'How can you say that?' he demanded. 'You're *beautiful*.'

She yanked her arms from his hold with a strength he wouldn't have believed from someone so slender and shoved at his chest again. 'You liar! And you know what? I'm a liar too. I *do* remember that night. I remember everything about it and God alone knows I've spent the past five years trying to move on with my life and forget my shame and the cruel things you said, but I *can't*. Your words and your disgust are stained in my memories, and for you to kiss me like that and call me beautiful… How can you do that to me? Why do you hate me so much…?'

He grasped her shoulders and pulled her to him. 'Are you insane? I don't *hate* you. I could never hate you, and you don't disgust me…'

A groan ripped from his throat as a wave of crippling self-loathing battered him.

'Don't you understand?' he implored with a roar. 'The disgust wasn't aimed at you. It was for *me*.'

Her eyes widened. A hitching sound came from her moving throat.

'When I found you there… Can't you understand what that was like for me? The position you put me in? This beautiful young woman inviting me… How could I have lived with myself if I'd taken advantage of what you were offering? You were *drunk*. And, Elsa, I owe your parents everything. They trusted me to look out for you and I would have sooner ripped my throat out than abuse that trust.'

A tear spilled down her cheek. He brushed it away with his thumb and pressed his forehead to hers, staring deep into her eyes. 'I'm sorry I hurt you, *chiquita*. I should have handled it much more sensitively, but I was too angry with you and furious with myself to think straight. I have never known temptation like that before…' Fingers spearing her silky hair, he brushed his lips lightly over hers. 'Not until you came back into my life. These past days have been torture. I know it's wrong but I ache for you. You're in my head all the time. All I want is to touch you.'

The tips of their noses rubbed, eyes locked together. Her hand tentatively inched up his arm and over his shoulder to the nape of his neck, her fingers brushing against the soft strands of his hair.

'Why is it wrong?' Her voice was throaty and barely audible. Her sweet breaths whispered against his lips, diving straight into his already overloaded senses.

He groaned again and fisted her hair, doing his mightiest to hold on, to remember all the reasons why he shouldn't do this.

What *were* they? He fought to remember, fought to resist…

The beats of Elsa's heart were so violent the echo slammed like a pulse in her head.

Had she fallen into a dream?

Was this really Santi leaning into her and staring at her as if she were someone to be worshipped? She could feel the tremors coming from his powerful body. Every part of her trembled too.

And then his lips crashed against hers. In the beat of a moment Elsa found herself crushed against him, his mouth devouring hers, tongues clashing as if trying to eat each other whole.

She had to be dreaming. This couldn't be real.

The scorching of her skin where his fingers and palms were sweeping over her back and sides, his touch penetrating the material of her dress, felt real. The brush of his beard against her cheek as his mouth devoured hers felt real too. The burning heat in her pelvis…

The feelings ricocheting through her, the *intensity* of them…

The groaning of her name as he severed the kiss but not the connection made her heart sing. She felt a delicious scratching along her throat as his cheek buried into it before her stomach dipped and she found herself being lifted into his arms and carried to the bed.

Santi laid her down gently. Her golden cheeks were flushed, her lips plumped from his kisses. Her chest was making rapid rise and fall movements. He rested the back of his fingers at the top of the slope of her left breast. The ragged beats of her heart drummed against them, perfectly matching those of his own.

All his nerves had gone crazy. He felt intoxicated. The world had become a blur, his only focus the woman staring at him with such heady wonder.

Slowly, he dragged his fingers down and over the swell of her breast, his thumb encircling the jut of her roused nipple through the fabric of her dress.

He felt her tremble. Heard the faint hitch in her throat. Her breaths had shortened to quick, erratic exhalations.

He could hardly breathe at all.

Taking great care not to put all his weight on her, Santi propped himself on his elbows to stare again into her mesmerising eyes. And then he kissed her, a long, deep hungry kiss that had her moaning into him and sliding a hand around his neck to pull him closer.

He dragged his mouth from hers and kissed and inhaled his way across her cheek and to her neck, ravenous to taste and touch every inch of her. Lower he inched until he reached the top line of her dress. The buttons were tiny and his strangely clumsy fingers had trouble undoing the first two, becoming only slightly more dextrous by the third.

When he reached the fourth button, Elsa felt a sudden tendril of trepidation and covered his hand tightly to stop him going any further. All the illumination in the cabin came from the moonlight flooding in through the large window.

'Close the blinds,' she whispered urgently. The intensity of her feelings were so strong she didn't want to lose them through fear.

His face hovered back over hers for a moment, black eyes boring into hers questioningly.

She palmed his cheek and rubbed the soft bristles of his beard, then lifted her head to kiss him. 'Please. Close them.'

A draught of coldness replaced the warmth of his body as he left her just long enough to release the blind at the side of the bed before the warmth returned with the enveloping darkness and Santi picked up where he'd left off, kissing her, exploring her body with his hands…

Elsa sank back into the pleasure he was eliciting in her.

'You're beautiful,' he whispered when he kissed the base of her throat. He opened the next two buttons of her dress and slipped a hand into the exposed part to cup one of her breasts, sending such a jolt of sensation through the sensitive flesh that she gasped.

More buttons were undone. He reached her abdomen. His fingers pushed beneath the lace of her panties and brushed over her sex, making her gasp again, this time with shock at the unexpectedness as well as the pleasure.

There was something in Elsa's gasp that set alarm bells ringing. Santi shuffled back up to gaze down at her, wishing she hadn't asked him to close the blinds so he could look at her clearly.

He stroked the soft skin of her cheek. 'Have you done this before?' he asked quietly before the question had even formed solidly in his mind.

She stilled in his arms. She hesitated then slowly shook her head.

His heart fell. A distant ringing played in his ears. A weight compressed his chest.

But there was another emotion at play too, one he could hardly bring himself to admit. Exhilaration.

Since that late summer morning when her naked silhouette had shone through the light streaming in the villa's kitchen window, Elsa had been a constant itch in Santi's psyche. He'd gone for months at a time—years—without seeing her but not a single day had gone by when he hadn't thought of her. He'd listen to her family's stories about her new life in Vienna and feel lightened to hear she was happy and thriving, but the lightness had masked the knotted heaviness in his guts that had been there since he'd woken the morning after kicking her out of his bed. The knots had always tightened at tales of Elsa's varied love life.

Those had been the times he'd sought release with other women, he now admitted to himself. Fleeting satisfaction to drive out the selfish ache in his heart at the thought of Elsa being with another man.

She hadn't been with anyone. He didn't dare dissect what he felt about that.

He brushed his fingers through her hair. 'We don't have to do this. We don't have to do anything.'

She touched his head and her fingers sank into the curls. 'Santi...' She sighed. Her voice was barely audible. 'It feels like I've waited my whole life for this.'

He squeezed his eyes shut and breathed deeply. At that moment in time, it felt like he'd waited his whole life for this too.

And then he took another step into the fire and kissed her again.

He'd never known kisses alone could fuel fire. The feel of Elsa's lips against his. Her sweet yet headily addictive taste. The scent of her skin. All of it took mere kissing to a whole new dimension of sensuality and at that moment he wouldn't have cared if she'd said she wanted to do nothing more than kiss. It would be enough.

Slowly, tenderly, he undressed her. There was no frustration in having to take things slowly despite arousal bleeding through his pores. For the first time perhaps in for ever he *wanted* to take his time, not just for Elsa but for himself. He wanted to savour each and every moment.

When Elsa was naked and under the covers, she watched Santi strip with a heart that felt like a hot air balloon threatening to burst out of her chest.

Once he was naked, he lay back on her. She wished she could put into words and share with him how incredible it felt to be living this moment…but then he kissed her with such tender passion that she *knew* those feelings were shared.

And then he kissed her some more. His lips left a burning trail over her body that felt like it was penetrating her skin, drugging her, turning her from a sentient person into a mass of nerve-endings and sensation. When he took her nipples into his mouth and cupped her throbbing core, she could no more stop her cries of ecstasy than a baby could stop its cries of hunger.

He trailed his way back to her mouth and kissed her with a passion that left her boneless then parted her thighs to accommodate his solid bulk. The even heftier weight of his arousal pressed against the lips of her opening.

His voice was thicker and huskier than she'd ever heard it when he said, 'We need protection.'

She dragged her fingers into his hair and whispered, 'I'm on the Pill.'

'You trust me?'

'Always.'

She'd thought her heart couldn't beat any harder than it already had but it smashed into her lungs and up to her throat, making her tremble with the strength of its reverberations.

This was it.

Santi rubbed his nose to hers and tried to breathe through the thuds of his heart. It felt like it was *his* first time.

But it was hers, and the magnitude of what they were about to do was not something he took lightly.

'When I found you on my bed all those years ago…' He brushed a light kiss to her mouth. 'Elsa, I have never in my life seen anything so beautiful.' He feathered slow kisses over her cheeks, over her eyelids, and pushed just the tip of his arousal inside her. 'You were—*are*—perfect.' He kissed her mouth again and drove a little further. 'Rejecting you was the hardest thing I have ever done.' There was only the slightest resistance before her tight, velvet warmth opened for him. He drove even further inside her and groaned at the undiluted pleasure of her muscles gripping him. He'd never known sensation like it.

Elsa had been so caught in Santi's magical words tasting like nectar to her senses and the explosions of heat pulsing through her that it wasn't until he stilled and moaned in her ear that she fully comprehended that he was inside her. Massively inside her, stretching her, filling her...

Dear sweet heaven...

The feelings that erupted in her were so deep and powerful that she cried out and hooked an arm around his neck.

He stiffened in her arms. 'Are you okay, *chiquita*? Do you want me to stop?'

Stop? He'd have to kill her first.

Her pelvis tilted with no input from her brain to deepen the penetration and then she was holding onto him with all her might, clinging to him, pressing and rocking, her head thrashing, no thoughts in her head, her body moving on pure instinct, desperate for the relief it knew only Santi could provide.

His hand clasped her bottom as he ground into her, increasing the friction, and then, without any warning, she shattered into a million pieces, torn apart by the waves of the most intense pleasure lashing and rupturing through her, barely aware that she was calling his name out over and over and over.

CHAPTER NINE

ELSA LAY WITH her head on Santi's chest, feeling the rhythmic beats of his heart against her ear. The soft hair on his chest tickled her cheek. There was a delicious lethargy in her limbs and a strange tingling sensation in her pelvis.

She didn't want to fall asleep. Didn't want to lose the wonder. Didn't want to wake and find the most magical night of her life had been a dream.

She'd lain there so long her arm was starting to seize up. Carefully, she disentangled herself and propped herself on an elbow. She could see the outline of his handsome face through the darkness and placed a gentle kiss to his mouth.

His head moved and he mumbled something. His hand groped for hers. She laced her fingers through his and pressed it against her heart. Could he hear its beats in his sleep?

Was he dreaming? Was *she* dreaming?

Only when her arm started to hurt again did she lie down and, wrapped snugly in his sleeping arms, finally close her eyes.

* * *

When Elsa next opened her eyes, it was to find the side of the bed Santi had slept on empty and dusky early light filtering through the blinds. She rolled onto her back and closed her eyes again.

What had he thought when he'd crept out of her bed? Had he already been regretting what they'd shared?

Was she?

She showered and dressed in record time, pausing only once to stand in front of the mirror with the towel around her. Santi had said she was beautiful. Were they just words given to appease an over-emotional woman? What did he really see when he looked at her?

Smoothing her oversized scoop-necked silver T-shirt over her black shorts, all ideas of playing it cool around him were lost when she found herself hesitating at the steps. She didn't have a clue how she was supposed to act. Was there a special etiquette for facing the man you'd made love to the morning after?

She didn't have a clue how he was going to act either, knew only that she needed to prepare herself for any outcome.

She forced her legs to climb the stairs and compelled the muscles on her face into a semblance of nonchalance.

Santi was busy fiddling with the coffee pot, wearing a pair of loose-fitting beige shorts and an unbuttoned short-sleeved black shirt.

Just to look at him was to knock all the wind from her.

Their eyes met. The silence between them was so complete that if a feather floated in the air, she'd be able to hear the barbs rustling through it. It took what felt like for ever for his mouth and eyes to crease into a smile.

'Good morning, *chiquita*,' he said softly.

She couldn't make her vocal cords work. All she could do was smile through the flaming of her cheeks and press herself against the dining table to support her weakening legs.

'Coffee?' he asked in the same soft tone.

She cleared her throat and managed to croak, 'Please.'

He removed a mug from a cupboard and placed it beside the one already set in front of him. 'I spoke to Felipe earlier,' he said in a more conversational tone. 'It will happen tomorrow.'

Elsa's head was so full of the man she'd spent the night with that it took her a moment to understand what he'd said. 'For sure?'

'First thing in the morning.' He poured coffee into the mugs. 'As soon as we have confirmation it's over, we can get the extraction plan in place and get you home.'

'Okay.' She didn't need to question him about it. Santi would never put her in harm's reach, and that was good enough for her.

It was emotional harm she had to be wary of. Especially now. Especially when she didn't have a clue what he was thinking or feeling and barely understood her own thoughts and emotions.

He carried the coffees to her, lips curved as held hers out.

A frisson sparked as their fingers brushed.

Nothing was said for the longest time. They faced each other by the table, gazes locked. The longer they stood there, the faster the beats of Elsa's heart became and the more ragged her breaths. She ached to touch him. Put her arms around his neck and kiss him. She ached for him to touch her too. More than all that, she wanted him to do or say something to ease the fear building inside her that they'd made a colossal mistake.

Just as she feared she would self-combust with all the emotions tearing through her, he put his mug on the table then plucked hers from her hand and placed it beside his own. Then he put his hands on her waist and pulled her to him. The relief was so great that for one frightening moment she feared she would cry from the magnitude of it.

He traced a finger over her cheek sending shivers of sensation racing through her. 'Any regrets?' he asked seriously.

How to answer that with his black eyes so intent on her? How to answer with such a jumble of emotions frothing in her?

She'd given her heart to Santi once and his rejection had shattered it and shaken the foundations of her happy, carefree life. Her father's death and the circumstances around it had ruptured the loosened foundations beyond repair. It had destroyed her faith and trust in *everything*.

To feel such joy in Santi's arms was dangerous, felt too much like the old, reckless way she'd thrown herself into experiences for the sheer exhilaration of it, blithely assuming she would fall on her feet or if she stumbled then never mind because Santi would be there to catch her and deliver her safely home.

That safety was gone. The lynchpin of her family was gone. Elsa had had no choice but to find safety on her own terms and under her own control. She'd made a life for herself. By no means could it be called exhilarating but it was safe…or had been until the cartel had reared its head again. She'd worked too hard to claw herself out of the black pit of terror and despair to risk ripping herself apart emotionally again.

She could trust Santi to catch her if she fell but she couldn't trust him with her heart again. Couldn't trust he'd give it back to her whole.

But to regret their night together?

She sighed and looped her arms around his neck, shaking her head in answer. Elsa couldn't regret something that had given her more pleasure in one night than she'd felt in the past five years combined. And she wasn't a naïve teenager any more, associating sex with love and love with for ever.

Santi had watched the conflicting emotions flitter over Elsa's beautiful face with his breath held.

When he'd woken, limbs entwined with Elsa's, her silky deep red hair splayed over his chest, everything they'd shared in the night had flashed before him and he'd been consumed with a wave of guilt and self-recrimination. And then he'd stared at her sleeping face and an even stronger wave of desire had blown the self-loathing away...and tenderness. Such tenderness.

He felt it now. The desire and the tenderness. The latter was an emotion he'd never felt before in his life, and he'd slipped out of her bed sickened with himself.

He couldn't wrap his head around her being a virgin. Was that the reason she'd been shy about him seeing her naked? Or did it run deeper? The girl who'd been happy to parade herself in a tiny bikini had grown into a woman who dressed conservatively and hadn't even stripped to a modest swimsuit during their time on the yacht. It sat heavily that the reason might have its roots in that long-ago night.

It made his heart clench to think that night had haunted her as much as it had haunted him. He'd spent five years believing she was getting on with her life and living it to the full. He'd been happy for her. He'd *wanted* Elsa to be happy. A happy Elsa could light a room with a smile.

But, with sunlight starting to filter through the windows, these were thoughts to be contemplated another time. His primary focus had to be on setting sail before the bay came to life. He would not drop his guard until he knew for certain that the danger to Elsa was over and that meant avoiding people in daylight.

'I need to raise the anchor and set our course,' he murmured, and, though he knew he shouldn't, was unable to resist placing a lingering chaste kiss to her lips and inhaling a brief taste of her sweetness.

Her head tilted back, exposing her beautiful throat. 'Can I help?'

'It's too light out there. Stay inside. Relax. I shouldn't be long.'

He stepped back, stroked her cheek one more time and walked out into the bright early morning light.

He breathed the fresh sea air deep into his lungs and tried to banish Marco's sad, reproachful face from his mind.

Censuring himself was pointless, he thought grimly. There would be plenty of time for self-recrimination once he'd delivered Elsa safely to her family. Until that time…

He'd just have to contain it as much as he could.

But something told him containing it was no longer possible. The genie was out of the bottle and couldn't be put back.

The moment Elsa was alone she sank onto the nearest seat and closed her eyes. Her pelvis tingled. Her veins buzzed. Her pulse whooshed in her ears. In her mind was the look in Santi's eyes when he'd traced his finger over her cheek. There had been emotion. Desire. The same look as she'd seen all those other times.

She hadn't imagined it.

A bubble of laughter rose up her throat, as uncontrollable as all the other feelings ravaging her, but then cut itself off as her brief rise of spirits crashed back down to earth.

A part of her, the old reckless Elsa, felt like she could

leap over mountains in single bounds. The other, newer, sensible Elsa screamed caution. Caution, caution, caution. Lock her heart tightly. Throw away the key. Don't let him anywhere near it.

But the buzz in her veins told her very clearly that if Santi tried to make love to her again, she would respond with the opposite of caution. Just to imagine it was to set the butterflies loose all over again.

Santi stared from the panini that had been placed on the ledge next to him at the helm of the yacht's sundeck to the woman who'd delivered it. 'Is that for me?'

Teenage Elsa had hated cooking and vowed never to learn. Something else that had changed about her.

Her beautiful hair flowed around her, no wig needed as there was no other vessel in their immediate vicinity. 'I thought you must be hungry. You only had a small breakfast.'

A small breakfast of fruit shared once they were on the open seas, interrupted by the constant pinging of the radar. This was the first moment of peace they'd had since they'd set sail three hours ago.

Touched, he put his hand on her hips and squeezed without thinking. 'Thank you.'

She smiled shyly and lightly, tentatively, ran her fingers through his hair. Then she stepped back. 'Aren't you going to try it?'

He picked up one of the wedges from the plate and took a huge bite…and immediately wished he hadn't.

Her face screwed up. 'Don't you like it?'

Fighting back his body's efforts to repel it, he forced his throat to swallow the bite. 'Not at all. Out of curiosity, what's in it?'

'Serrano ham and salad stuff. Tomatoes, peppers, those pickled things you like…'

That's what the taste was! 'Gherkins?'

She nodded. 'I thought that as they go well with burgers, they'd be nice in a panini.'

Not a whole jar of them! he wanted to say, but kept it to himself. She'd gone to the effort of making him something and he wasn't going to hurt her feelings by telling her it was inedible.

With Elsa's watchful eyes on him, he took another bite and chewed as little as he could before swallowing.

Her whole face lit up in a beaming smile. 'I'll pour the coffee and join you.'

The moment she disappeared from view, he gave a silent apology to the fish and chucked what was left of the panini into the sea, then grabbed the bottle of water by his foot and downed it to wash the taste out of his mouth.

Confident the yacht's co-ordinates were set properly, he set the autopilot and was about to rise to his feet when Elsa bounded up the steps scowling…

Well, her mouth was scowling. Her eyes were dancing with a mischievous light he hadn't seen in five years.

Putting her hands on her hips, she shook her mock-scowling face. 'You're such a liar! You said you liked the panini. I made one for myself and it's the most disgusting thing I've ever tasted!'

His lips twitched. 'I never said I liked it.'

'You said… Oh.' She stuck her bottom lip out and folded her arms in mock anger, but then lines creased her beautiful face and she burst into a peal of laughter so infectious that Santi found himself laughing too, and all the awkwardness that had lingered between them since early morning vanished.

Taking hold of her hips, he pulled her to him. The size difference between them was such that with him seated and her standing, they were the same height. 'How does a woman reach the age of twenty-three without knowing how to make a sandwich?'

'I *do* know.' She sniggered, looping her arms around his neck. 'I just made the mistake of trying to impress you with something fancier than serrano ham and tomato.'

'I'm touched…' He kissed her lightly, even though he knew he shouldn't. 'Please don't do it again.'

'I won't.' She gazed into his eyes, smiling, then her eyes clocked his empty plate and narrowed. 'Don't tell me you finished yours?'

'I fed it to the fish.'

'Poor fish. I'll make us something else.'

'No! *I'll* make lunch.' He spoke with such force that Elsa burst into another peal of laughter.

God, she was beautiful when she laughed. Her head tilted back, elongating the elegant arch of her neck, and he was suddenly engulfed in the heady fantasy of sinking his teeth into the golden skin…

Arousal shot through him so sharply his fingers tightened their grip on her hips.

She caught his eye and her laughter abruptly stopped.

For a long, long moment they did nothing but gaze into each other's eyes until suddenly their arms wound around each other and their mouths fused together in a kiss of such hunger that Santi was immediately consumed by it.

His hands slipping up her caftan to touch the silk of her heated skin; his last coherent thought before the pleasure took control was that he was already going to hell. Making love to her again couldn't add to his sentence.

Elsa sat at the sundeck's dining table with her face tilted to the sun. Every cell in her body tingled with the aftereffects of their sudden lovemaking.

She was beyond regrets. Regrets were pointless.

Couldn't she satisfy both parts of herself? she wondered. Couldn't she embrace this seductive desire that made her feel more alive than she'd felt in so, so long without losing the essence of herself and still protect her heart? Keep it locked tightly away? They had so little time left. The only thing stopping her going mad with fear for what tomorrow could bring was Santi. Tomorrow, her world could turn on its wheel again. It could be ripped apart at the seams.

If all she had was today then she wanted to live it.

Santi appeared from below deck with a tray. He winked at her, then unloaded two plates filled with the most beautifully presented tuna salad, a bowl of black olives, slices of warmed crusty bread, olive oil and a jug of iced water onto the table.

'This looks amazing,' she said.

'It's nothing. It took me ten minutes to prepare.'

'Don't be so modest. If I made something like this it'd end up looking like something Rocco would eat.'

His deep rumble of laughter made her belly go all squidgy. The little whorls of exposed hair on his chest— he'd put a white short-sleeved shirt on—made the rest of her go all squidgy too. Remembering how that hair felt against her cheek made her pelvis contract, and she hurriedly pressed her thighs together.

She'd been a virgin only a day ago and now all she could think of was sex?

She had her first bite of the salad. Her tastebuds pinged. Aromatic and lemony, the avocados giving it creaminess, the chickpeas giving it bite, it was delicious, and she told him so, adding, 'How come you're such a good cook?'

'My mother taught me. She believed everyone, man or woman, should be able to feed themselves, no matter how poor they were.'

'Were you poor?' All Elsa knew of Santi's early life was that he'd spent his first ten years in Seville.

'Very. My mother was only seventeen when she had me. She had no qualifications so had to work her backside off doing menial work to put food on the table. All our clothes came from the church's charity box. The car she drove was falling to pieces and she could never have afforded to replace it.' His smile had a faraway look. 'She never complained. She just got on.'

As hard as she tried, she couldn't picture Santi as a child. 'It was just the two of you, wasn't it?' That was something she'd always known, although she didn't remember how.

'Yes. My father died before I was born. A motorbike accident.'

'How horrible,' she said softly. 'Did you have much to do with his family?'

He swallowed his food and shook his head. 'Not since I was a baby. My mother had a big falling out with them. Her family were too busy trying to scrape a living themselves to help her much so it was mostly just the two of us until we moved to Valencia.'

'Was that for the job with my parents?'

'Yes.' He broke off a hunk of bread and used it to mop some of the dressing clinging to his plate. 'She wanted a fresh start for me. The area we lived in was rough. The school I went to was rough—lots of little thugs in the making, and I was one of them. She wanted a better life for me. When she saw the advert for a housekeeper in Valencia, she applied thinking she had nothing to lose.'

'How did you feel about the move?'

He shrugged. 'I had my *mamá*, so I didn't care where we lived. We were tight.' He crossed his fingers for emphasis.

Elsa drank some water thinking this explained so

much. No wonder Santi had gone so badly off the rails after she'd died. 'I wish I remembered her better.'

'You were very young when she died. She adored you.'

'Did she?'

His mouth widened into a huge smile that made her belly flip. 'You would toddle after her while she worked, trying to "help". You had a toy vacuum cleaner and would drag it all over the villa, following her... She missed you when you started infant school.'

A flash of memory made Elsa's windpipe close. Her first day of school. Conchita enveloping her in the biggest hug and telling her to have fun.

She stared at Santi and an almost unbearable wave of sadness hit her. 'I'm sorry you lost her so young.'

'So am I.' His gaze penetrated through the shades they both wore, the intensity strong enough for her veins to turn to sludge. 'I would never have got through it without your parents.'

'What did they do?'

'Don't you remember?'

She shook her head.

'When my mother was ill, they were there for us every step of the way. They took her to all her appointments and treatments, kept her on her full wages even though she wasn't well enough to work, and they looked after me. They made sure I ate. Had clean clothes. Attended school. That kind of thing. When she died, they sat me down and gave me two options. I could live with my *mamá*'s family in Seville and they would pay her wages to support me until I finished my education, or

I could stay in the housekeeper's cottage and live as a member of your family.'

'You chose us over your family?'

Santi shrugged. In his mother's year-long battle with cancer, not one member of his maternal family had made the effort to visit her. Not one hospital visit. All had cited the distance as their excuse, as if a six-and-a-half-hour drive on the country's excellent *autopistas* was a trek through the Himalayan Mountains. His grandmother, who'd had mobility problems, had been the only one to attend the funeral. He only looked out for her now because he knew that's what his mother would want.

He condensed his reasons to, 'They'd come to be strangers to me.'

She asked the obvious question. 'Why didn't you move into the villa with us? You were only fifteen.'

Because, for all their kindness and empathy, I was a rough, ill-mannered boy who didn't belong in the rarefied world your family inhabited.

Just thinking such thoughts made him feel like a traitor but he had no illusions about where he belonged. The Lopezes' world was one of riches and elegance. A whole world away from his.

Knowing his private thoughts would hurt her, he settled on, 'Because your parents foresaw that I would turn into the teenager from hell and wanted to protect you and Marisa from it.' His eyes found hers again and his lips twitched. 'They should have taken up fortune-telling. The rest you know.'

He waited for Elsa to say or ask something else, but she looked troubled.

'What's wrong, *chiquita*?'

She sighed and put her elbow on the table to rest her cheek on her palm.

'You must have thought I was the biggest brat in the world,' Elsa said heavily.

A crease formed in his brow.

'All that time I spent complaining about my parents and the general unfairness of adolescent life when I had *nothing* to complain about,' she explained. Santi had always humoured her whining. Given sensible advice when needed. Sympathised. Told her to pull her head out of her bottom when her whining got too much.

If she'd been a little less self-absorbed in those years when he'd been her chauffeur, protector and friend, he might have opened up to her about his life.

To her relief, his eyes crinkled and he laughed. 'Your complaints were always entertaining.'

'But how did you put *up* with me?'

'Because you, *chiquita*, were *always* entertaining. Even when you were whining. And you know something else?'

She shook her head, fascinated at the change of expression on his face and the sensual tone that had entered his voice.

He stood up and leaned over the table. His breath was hot on her face as he growled, 'You're still entertaining but in a *very* different way. Now come here.'

CHAPTER TEN

SANTI PULLED OUT the cushions that transformed the area forward of the helm into a huge sunbathing area and lay down, then patted the space beside him. Elsa removed her sunhat with the shy smile he was becoming used to and curled into him. Beneath her caftan, she was naked.

For the longest time they did nothing but lie there curled together. Her knee slipped between his thighs. After carrying her to his cabin and making love to her again, he'd thought he was too sated to feel arousal again so soon but heat trickled into his loins, slowly, deliciously.

Desire. Pulled out of the shadows they'd both boxed it into and shining brightly like dancing fire.

Desire. Out in the open. No longer deniable. No longer denied.

He'd touched the fire and let it enflame him.

It would extinguish itself when they returned to Valencia.

'I need to ask you something,' he said before his arousal could take control of all his senses again. There were things he needed to know before their time together came to an end.

He heard her long intake of breath before she raised her face to look into his eyes. 'Go on.'

'That night. Was it the reason you moved to Vienna?'

It struck him then that he already knew the answer. He'd always known, just refused to acknowledge it. Within a fortnight of that haunting night, Elsa had gone.

Her stare held his. It seemed like a thousand emotions rang out at him.

Guilt pressed into his guts. 'I really hurt you, didn't I.'

It wasn't a question.

Hating the self-recrimination she could feel vibrating from him, Elsa traced the chain around his neck with her finger. 'Yes, but the blame never lay with you—it was all on me. I felt such *shame*.'

Until they'd given voice to the elephant in the room that had been there from their first clash of eyes in Vienna, Elsa had never thought about that night from Santi's perspective. Or how he'd asked her to leave numerous times and she'd blithely ignored him, going as far as to try to drag him onto the bed when *he*'d tried to leave the room.

All she'd remembered with any clarity had been his cruel words and the look of disgust on his face. The lancing sting of his rejection.

'Your rejection… That was the first real rejection of my life. I was so spoilt—'

'No,' he cut in. 'You weren't spoilt. You never looked down on people.'

'Thank you, but I *was* spoilt. I had the happiest childhood. Life was one big adventure and it felt that the world turned just for *me*. Your rejection was a sharp lesson in the reality of life and the first time there had been a real consequence to my actions, but I didn't have the emotional tools or maturity to handle it so, yes, I did move to Vienna to escape you. I didn't think I could bear to see you again.'

His hand tightened around hers. 'I'm sorry.'

'Don't be. It was for the best. I needed a fresh start. I needed to grow up and learn to fend for myself. I needed to learn independence.'

'Then why didn't you learn to cook?' he teased.

'Stubbornness,' she said, glad of the lightening of tone.

He rested a hand on her hip and pulled her even tighter to him. 'I get why you needed a fresh start but why did that have to mean you turning into a loner?' Because Santi was convinced Elsa's Vienna years had been mostly spent alone. It hurt his heart to think of the vivacious young woman who'd thrived on company being by herself all that time.

'It wasn't intentional but my fresh start meant turning my back on the things that had got me into trouble, namely alcohol. How I behaved that night... I can't blame the alcohol, those were *my* actions, but all that rum...it made me lose my inhibitions completely and I was terrified of it happening again. I felt like I was a runaway train falling head first off the track and the only way to stop it was to slam my foot on the brakes. I didn't go to any of the parties I was invited to and eventually people stopped asking. If you can believe it, I was known as a goody-goody at university.'

He feigned shock. '*No!* Elsa Lopez a goody-goody?'

'They think I'm a goody-goody at work too.'

'Does that bother you?'

'Sometimes. When I overhear colleagues make plans for a night out I'm not invited to.'

He heard the wistfulness in her voice and fell silent for a moment. 'Has hiding away from life made you happy?'

'It's never felt like hiding away. More like self-preservation.'

'Okay, but has it made you happy?' he persisted.

Her silence gave the answer to that.

'Why didn't you come home?' he asked quietly.

'I don't know,' she whispered. 'I suppose…' Elsa sighed and rolled onto her back. A gull flew high over the yacht. She wondered if it ever felt exhilaration when it swooped through the air. She hoped it did. Hoped it was capable of appreciating the freedom its wings gave it. Elsa used to wish for wings. She remembered being about four or five and climbing on the roof of the villa wearing her dressing-up fairy wings. She'd been convinced they would make her fly.

If Marisa hadn't followed her up and screamed for their *mamá* to stop her, she would have jumped. If her mama hadn't then thrown the fairy wings away, she would have tried again when no one was looking. Luckily, her faith in the magic of her fairy wings had stopped her trying without them until she'd jumped off that cliff thirteen years later.

She envied her younger self. She'd been free in her heart.

'When I'm in Vienna, I wear this persona,' she said quietly. 'People there accept me as this hard-working, strait-laced young woman and I can *be* that woman. There's no temptation. It's safe. *I'm* safe. And in control of myself and my life.'

'But not happy.'

'No,' she admitted reluctantly. 'I think I've forgotten how to be happy. Especially since Papá…'

Her throat hitched as her voice trailed off. The sound of her pain made Santi's heart cramp tightly and he had to suck in a breath to loosen it.

'You know what you need to do when all this is over, Elsa?' he said, breaking the sudden cloud of grief that had shrouded them, wanting, *needing*, to see her smile.

Her eyes held his starkly. 'What?'

'Let it go.'

It took a moment for the old joke he used to throw at her when she was in a particularly whiny mood to sink in. It was worth the wait. Her melancholy expression dissolved, her face creasing as she spluttered with laughter.

'If you start singing, I'm going to cook something and force-feed it to you,' she threatened.

'No singing, I promise,' he said quickly, making her snigger even more.

He propped himself on an elbow to gaze down at her beautiful face. 'But you do need to put it behind you.

You can't let shame over an incident when you were only eighteen make you hide away from life for ever. You're a grown woman. If you want a rum and Coke, what's wrong with that? You're perfectly capable of stopping before you get close to losing your inhibitions. And if you don't want to drink, why let that stop you from partying? Do you really want to look at yourself when you're a little old lady and say, "I had some great times sitting at my office desk"?'

As he spoke, Santi had to acknowledge that the latter part of his advice could equally apply to him. When had he last taken time away from his business and simply lived for the moment?

The answer came to him immediately. Elsa's eighteenth birthday party.

It shocked him to know that really had been it. Five whole years without a break. He'd forgotten how good it felt to relax and do nothing, to simply enjoy being alive.

Right then, he felt more alive than he'd ever done. Every cell in his body was awake and zinging. Tomorrow they would be back in Valencia and this brief flare of passion between them would be over.

Covering her with his body, he kissed her. 'You're beautiful, Elsa Lopez.' He ran a hand over the contours of her incredible body. 'And sexy. *Very* sexy.' He cupped a breast and grazed his teeth over her neck, then took her hand to guide it to his arousal. Her gasp followed by a soft moan only made him harder. 'Feel what you do to me,' he breathed. 'This is all you.'

And then he showed her exactly what she did to him.

* * *

Elsa wrinkled her nose at the array of vegetables laid out on the kitchen counter. 'What are we making?'

After anchoring at sea for the night, Santi had announced it was time for her first cooking lesson. She'd agreed only because she couldn't think of a good reason not to.

'Pisto.'

Her mouth watered at the thought. She loved the Spanish take on ratatouille.

He picked a kitchen knife up and held it out to her, handle first. 'Your first job is to slice the onions.'

She took hold of the knife gingerly and stared at the onion, wondering if she was supposed to take the outer brown layer off first.

'Shall I show you how to do it?' he asked.

As there was no point pretending she had a clue what she was doing, she happily stepped aside.

Her mouth dropped open to witness Santi tackle the onion. For a man whose hands could easily be classified as bear paws without the hairiness, he had a deftness of touch and in less than a minute the onion was peeled and professionally sliced.

Done, he raised an eyebrow. 'Do you need me to show you how to dice a pepper too?'

Thinking of the way she'd massacred the pepper she'd chopped for their paninis, she laughed. 'Probably a good idea.'

He stretched an arm in front of her and grabbed a red one. The movement set off a wave of his cologne and in an instant Elsa's senses were filled with the scent of Santi. She leaned in closer.

'Here. Hold it like this and… *Chiquita*, what are you doing?'

'Sniffing you.' She slipped an arm around his waist, only to be deterred by his hand.

'No,' he said sternly. 'You are not going to seduce me into stopping your cooking lesson. I'm teaching you a valuable life lesson.'

'Can't you teach me another time?'

He lightly tapped the tip of her nose. 'Watch and learn.'

'I can learn when I get back to Vienna.'

'Schnitzel?' He laughed.

'It's actually nice. You should try it one day.' She almost added, 'with me', but quickly stopped herself. What was happening to them was nothing but lust. If it turned into something more then…

No, she would not think like that. She would not go there. She would not allow her mind to conjure delusions and spoil the happiness of today.

Music was playing and a song she liked came over the system. She tapped her foot along to the beat. If not for the gnawing fear of what tomorrow could bring, she thought this might be the happiest she'd felt in a long, long time.

She shoved aside the nagging voice that her fears for tomorrow were not only to do with her family's safety.

Her heart was safely enclosed and if she felt it straining for freedom, she simply tightened the lock around

it. That was a valuable life lesson she'd taught herself...
hadn't she...?

Shaking all the unwanted thoughts away, she peered
at the chopping board now piled high with an array of
vegetables. 'When did you last cook before this trip?'
she asked.

He shrugged. 'Years ago.'

'You enjoy it?'

'Very much. It's therapeutic.'

'Then why employ a chef?'

He thought about this too as he continued to dice. 'I
don't have time to cook. I work twelve-hour days mini-
mum and travel a great deal.'

She watched him pull a pan out of a cupboard and
felt the strangest welling of pride for him. 'You're incredible, do you know that?'

She only realised she'd spoken aloud when he raised a
disbelieving brow and she hurriedly clarified, 'The success you've made of yourself. Our family business took
decades to become as profitable as it is today but you
achieved ten times as much in a fraction of the time.'

'I couldn't have done it without your father.'

'He helped, I'm sure, but it was your hard work that
did it, so stop being modest. It doesn't suit you,' she
added with a cackle.

Santi laughed at the delight on Elsa's face. How wonderful it was to see the joyful girl he'd known seeping
out of the adult woman, as if she'd been hiding inside
and just waiting to come back to life.

He'd laughed more these last few days than he'd laughed in years too.

When had he become so serious? He supposed the more pertinent question would be *why*.

He'd never set out to earn himself a fortune. He'd simply wanted to make something of himself and make the family who'd given him so much proud. His business model had been a hit and he'd quickly gained a reputation for honesty and reliability. Word of mouth had done more to boost his business than any advertising. Businesses trusted him to transport their goods across the world in a timely fashion and without damage to their stock.

More wants more, his mother had often said. He supposed there was something in that. The more his business grew, the greater his ambitions. The more he'd earned, the more he'd wanted to earn. As his wealth had grown so too had the trappings he'd purchased to go with it, none of which he'd actually taken the time to enjoy.

He poured a little olive oil in the pan. 'Now the vegetables are ready, we can start cooking. We start by sautéing the onion.'

'Sautéing?'

'Frying.'

'Why didn't you just say that?'

'Do you want to learn or not?'

Her face was completely deadpan. 'Not.'

He shook his head, amusement building back up again. 'You're lucky we're living in modern times where you're not chained to the kitchen.'

'I'd chew my way through the chains to escape.'

'I can well believe it. How have you not starved these last five years?'

'Restaurants, cafés and takeaways.' Then she added brightly, 'Marisa's gone all maternal and taught herself to cook baby food for Nikos.'

'Good for her.'

She laughed. 'She made sure Raul knows she won't cook for him.'

'I'm sure he was devastated.'

'Not devastated enough to end the engagement.'

'You really don't like him, do you?'

'Neither do you,' she reminded him. 'You know, when Marisa first said she wanted to get married, I thought she'd ask you.'

He turned his face to her. 'You thought Marisa would ask *me* to marry her?'

'It makes sense.' Elsa said airily. See, she told herself triumphantly, her heart was *fine*. Those months spent fighting cold sweats and living with the tightest cramping feeling in her stomach as she'd waited for the day her sister's thoughts aligned with her own had been nothing but echoes of her old obsession with him. Santi marrying Marisa had been an excellent idea because it meant her sister and nephew would have had someone with their best interests at heart.

If she'd almost fainted with relief when Marisa had announced she would marry Raul... Well, that was just another echo too.

'She's after a business partner for herself and a father for her son,' she said. 'You're practically family. You know every aspect of our business inside out. To be honest, I'm surprised you didn't suggest it to her.'

'The thought never crossed my mind.' Not for a second. Santi liked Marisa, was as protective of her as he was the rest of the Lopezes but they'd never bonded the way he and Elsa had.

His heart made a sudden lurch to imagine Elsa in Marisa's situation. The father of her child dead. Her father murdered. Expected to take over a multi-national corporation. A dangerous cartel doing everything in its power to drag the business into its nefarious dealings.

He couldn't escape the sinking feeling that had it been Elsa in Marisa's shoes, he would have been by her side in an instant with the biggest gun he could get his hands on and never let her out of his sight for a moment. He would have insisted she marry him and to hell with the consequences.

'I don't think your *mamá* would be happy for me to marry her daughter,' he commented through a throat that felt as if it had broken glass in it.

'What makes you say that?'

He tried to keep his tone light. '*Chiquita*, Lopez blood is blue. Rodriguez blood is red.'

'All blood is red.'

'I was speaking figuratively.'

'And I was speaking factually. Mamá loves and trusts you.'

Not enough to have allowed him to move into the main villa after his own mother had died, he thought, but kept that to himself. He felt bad enough thinking it, let alone vocalising it.

But he knew that for all Rosaria loved and trusted him, she would never consider him a good life match for one of her precious daughters. Marco wouldn't have either. Santi was like a stray fighting dog they'd taken in, fed, sheltered, taught to obey and protect its owner but with the owner always having a healthy respect for the dog's inherent nature. The dog had been one wrong move away from being metaphorically put down.

Rosaria, like her late husband, knew everything about Santi. She'd seen him at his worst. She'd supported him and treated him like he was of her blood… But he was still that stray dog.

He had made it to the very top. He'd reached an unimaginable level of success and wealth. He was good enough for anyone, and anyone who disagreed could kiss his backside. But in his heart he knew he wasn't good enough for the Lopez girls. The world he'd come to inhabit was their natural home. They belonged to it. He was the interloper tolerated only because of his wealth.

When this situation was over and he and Elsa returned to their normal lives, he would have to face the guilt of knowing he'd abused the trust Rosaria had put in him. He would have to visit Marco's grave knowing he'd be turning in it at the thought of Santi touching his precious daughter.

CHAPTER ELEVEN

ELSA KEPT HAVING to remind herself to breathe. She couldn't stop her fingers drumming on the dining table or stop her legs from shaking. She'd been a wreck from the moment her eyes had snapped open at the unholy hour of five a.m.

The cartel was being taken down. It was happening right now.

Until she'd woken that morning, being on the yacht with Santi had dulled her panic. His confidence and assurance that there would be no danger to her family had rubbed off on her and she'd spent their time sailing the Mediterranean falling under his spell rather than flaying her skin with worry.

If she hadn't had his calm presence with her now, she would likely have torn out every hair on her head.

As time ticked slowly on, she couldn't stop her mind veering wildly to imagine it all going wrong. She'd lost her father to this murderous group and now she couldn't stop thinking of her mother, sister and nephew all in the firing line, even though she knew that was ridiculous and the action would be taking place far from the Lopez estate.

But what if the cartel had a contingency in place to swarm the villa and take her family hostage?

The what-ifs were never-ending.

Her wild ruminations were interrupted when Santi placed a plate full of pastries on the table and ruffled her hair with a gentle, 'Eat.'

'I'm not hungry,' she whispered. Her stomach and throat were so constricted she'd struggled to swallow the endless cups of coffee he kept making for her.

He stood behind her and laid his strong hands on her shoulders 'You need to keep your strength up,' he murmured, massaging her tense muscles. 'We might not hear anything for hours.'

She closed her eyes as a little of the tension racking her lessened. Only because he'd gone to the effort of preparing them for her did she eventually rip off a piece of pastry and pop it in her mouth. She might as well be eating cardboard. Did stress affect the tastebuds?

Elsa was about to swallow the last bit of pastry when Santi's phone rang.

Every part of her froze.

The hands still kneading her neck and shoulders froze too, but only for a moment.

Calmly, he picked the phone up from the table, swiped to accept the call, and put it to his ear. 'Felipe,' he said by way of greeting.

Elsa watched his reactions intently, searching for a sign, a tell, anything.

His eyes met hers. He nodded, lips curving into a smile.

She slumped in her seat and pressed a hand to her racing chest, and finally managed to exhale her pent-up breath.

Thank you, God. Thank you. Thank you.

Her own phone rang, pulling her out of her over-whelmed daze.

'Mamá?'

'It's over, darling. We're safe.'

Elsa pinched the bridge of her nose to stifle the threatening tears. 'You're really safe?'

'I swear.' Her voice lowered. 'I know how hard this must have been for you but it's over, and when I see you tomorrow I will—'

'Tomorrow? I thought there was an extraction plan to bring me home immediately?'

'There is, darling, but we were moved to a safe house in Geneva yesterday—'

'*What*?' Her gaze flew back to Santi, who was still discussing things with Felipe.

'It was a last-minute precaution taken by Felipe. Poor Nikos is teething and the flight hurt his ears so he had a terrible night and your sister hasn't slept. We can't put him through another flight, so we're going to drive back and stay in a hotel for the night. We'll be home in the morning.'

Until that moment, Elsa hadn't realised how desper-ate she was to be with her family and the guilt she felt at not being with them throughout the whole ordeal.

'I'm sorry I wasn't there with you,' she said quietly, sniffing back more tears.

'We'll be together again in the morning,' her mother promised, then her voice lowered. 'How have things been with Santi?'

Feeling her cheeks redden at the mention of his name, Elsa twisted to face the window so he couldn't see. 'Fine. Fine.'

'It made such a difference to Marisa and I, knowing you were in his care. It meant we could stop worrying about you. I do hope you two have resolved the...' she paused. '...differences between you.'

Elsa was very glad she'd turned her back to him for her mouth dropped open.

Her mother knew? Surely her father hadn't betrayed her confidence?

'I remember how your eyes always lit up when he walked into a room,' her mother said wistfully. 'I always hoped...'

'Hoped what?' she croaked when her mother's words hung in the air.

'That you would find your way back to him.'

A loud swoosh flew through her ears, like a wave crashing onto rocks. She pressed her burning forehead to the cool window and tried to think of something to say but her head was a jumble.

'I have to go,' her mother said. 'Have a safe journey home and I'll see you in the morning. I love you.'

Elsa's hands were shaking so hard she struggled to disconnect the call.

'Was that Marisa?' Santi asked. He'd been watching Elsa for the last minute, had seen her shudder and press her face against the window as if she'd been given bad news.

She shook her head. 'Mamá. They're safe.'

Then she burst into tears.

Sliding into the seat beside her, Santi hauled her into his arms and let her sob her relief, stroking her hair and kissing the top of her head until the tears ran dry.

'I can't believe it's finally over,' she mumbled into his chest, then tilted her face up at him. 'It *is* over, isn't it?'

'Yes, *chiquita*.' He bent his head and kissed her. 'It's over. All the leading members of the cartel have been arrested and their operations shut down. A handful of the lesser ranks in Naples escaped but they're powerless.' At least, he hoped they were. In the scheme of things, these four men and one woman were nothing but Santi suspected he wouldn't sleep properly until they were caught too. An international manhunt had already been launched to find them.

She nestled her face back against his chest and whispered, 'Thank you. For everything.'

He tightened his hold around her and pressed his mouth tightly to the top of her head.

Beats of dread ticked loudly in him. The time when he had to say goodbye to her, to let Elsa go, had accelerated with one phone call.

'Felipe's team will be here in around an hour. We should get our stuff together.' But he made no effort to disentangle his arms. This might be the last time he got to hold her like this.

She gave a long sigh then straightened and hooked her arms around his neck while wriggling onto his lap. Her nails grazed the bristles of hair on the nape of his neck. 'Felipe had Mamá and Marisa taken to Switzerland.'

'It was a last-minute judgement call.' He gathered her beautiful hair into his fist. 'I would have told you if I'd known.'

'They're safe. That's all that matters.' Her smile had a touch of melancholy to it but then her mesmerising eyes glittered with a hint of mischief. 'They won't be home until the morning…' Her hand drifted from his neck to palm his cheek. 'If we're extracted now we'll only be returning to an empty house…'

He stared into the green-brown depths, his heart inflating as her meaning became clear. 'You want me to call off the extraction?'

'Do you?'

Another day and night with Elsa? The thought alone was enough to put him into a state of instant arousal so hot it burned through any voice of caution. 'I think I could be persuaded.'

She kissed him with a hard, ferocious passion that stole his breath, pressing every inch of herself that should could into him as if she were trying to burrow into his skin.

When they finally came up for air, arms still locked around his neck, she gave the most contented smile. 'Did that persuade you?'

He pretended to ponder.

Her teeth grazed his neck then, before he could guess what she intended, she slithered off his lap and dropped to her knees so her face was level with his crotch. Grinning wickedly, she put her fingers to the top button of his shorts. 'Let's see if this persuades you.'

No longer having to keep an inner ear and eye alert to danger meant that for the first time since he'd embarked on this remarkable journey, Santi was able to fully relax.

After Elsa had used her very recently gained talents to persuade him to spend one last day on the yacht with her, he'd called the extraction off and arranged for his private jet to collect them on the island of Mallorca in the morning. And then he'd carried her to his cabin and made love to her with nothing more than his tongue. His loins twitched every time he remembered her throaty moans of pleasure. They'd then moved to the sundeck and carried on in much the same fashion.

With the sun's descent telling him better than his watch that evening was fast approaching, his loins twitched again to see her now, as naked as the day she was born, face in profile, lying on her stomach, dozing. The successful takedown of the cartel had taken the worry off her shoulders. She'd had a spring in her step ever since, a carefree joy that was utterly infectious. How could anyone not to be in such vibrant company? This was the Elsa he'd always imagined she would mature into, but with a mountain of sexiness.

'How would you like to go out tonight?' he asked,

tracing a finger down her spine, loving the way she shivered at his touch. 'Celebrate. Make the most of our last night together like this. Go for a meal and see where the night takes us.'

She lifted her head. The light in her eyes dazzled him before she gave a beaming smile that could have knocked him out with its power. 'I would love that.'

'We should think about putting some clothes on.' He cupped her smooth butt cheek. 'I would hate for a passing captain to train his binoculars on us and fall overboard with lust when he spied your perfect bottom.'

Her eyes pulsed. The lock of their gazes only broke when Elsa turned away and sat up with her back to him while she slipped her dress over her head. It pained him that despite everything they'd been through, she was still shy about her body around him. They'd spent hours naked yet she still pressed her thighs together and leaned forward and covered her breasts with an arm when doing something as simple as taking a drink of water.

Time and patience would, he was certain, see her lose the last of her inhibitions. But he wouldn't be the man to witness the final act of her blossoming. Come the morning and they would be over. The knife had barely penetrated his heart at this thought when she scrambled over to him and straddled his lap. The hem of her sundress bunched around her hips.

'Am I decent now?' she asked, fluttering her eyelashes.

He clasped her delectable bottom and mock-growled,

'Too decent.' His arousal thickened as she teased the folds of her sex over it. 'I much prefer you indecent.'

'Oh, do you?' She smiled innocently and sank down on him.

He groaned loudly at the all-engulfing pleasure and tightened his grip.

She pressed her cheek against his, raised herself then sank back down again. 'Is this indecent enough?'

He tried to capture her mouth in a kiss but was foiled when she suddenly sprang to her feet and took three quick steps away. Looking back over her shoulder, she said in the airiest of tones, 'I'm going to take a shower. Let me know if you need my help at the marina.'

Stunned, he pointed at the missile sprouting between his legs. 'You're going to leave me like this?'

She winked. 'I would hate to be responsible for a spike in boat accidents.'

Then she strode away, wriggling her bottom, leaving Santi with no choice but to laugh at her sheer provocativeness.

Elsa looked at her appearance and pulled a critical face. This was her first official date with Santi and she was dressed appropriately for a convent. She knew Santi wouldn't care what she wore but…

She froze on the spot.

Santi wouldn't care what she wore.

She could almost hear him. '*Chiquita*, you're beautiful whatever you wear.'

He thought she was beautiful. And it wasn't just

words. It was in the way he touched her. The way he kissed her. The way he looked at her...

Her heart vibrated in a sigh.

With barely conscious thought, Elsa tugged the zip at the side of the dress down and then pulled it over her head and threw it onto the floor.

Eyes glued to the mirror, she removed her underwear and gazed at her naked reflection properly for the first time in five years.

The compulsion to weep hit her so suddenly that her whole body contracted from the force of holding it back.

She would not let anything ruin this evening. This was an evening for celebration. The nightmare was over, her family were safe and she and Santi were embarking on something that might—and she was scared to jinx it by vocalising it even to herself—just might be the start of *something*.

But, still, she stared at her naked body and fought the tears as she finally accepted what her eyes were telling her, that she wasn't ugly, that her body was...just a body. No uglier or prettier than the average female body but beautiful in Santi's eyes.

Her chest feeling pierced with lightness, she opened the cupboard she'd stored her suitcase in and laid it on the bed. Inside it, having been stubbornly ignored since she'd first seen them at Santi's lodge...oh, but that felt like a lifetime ago...were the dresses Marisa had loaned her.

Santi was right. It was time to let the past go.

* * *

From as far back as he could remember, Santi had thought childhood cartoons where the rabbit or cat or dog or whatever's eyes popped out were ludicrous. That was until Elsa emerged from the cabin. His eyes might not be able to physically pop out but his jaw could certainly drop, and it did.

She held her hands out to the sides as she gave a quick twirl. 'Well? Will I do?'

Closing his mouth with a snap, he had to swallow a number of times to get some moisture going. '*Chiquita*, I'm going to be the envy of every red-blooded man in Mallorca tonight. You look…'

Like fire.

She wore a silk dusky rose, overlaid with gold lace wraparound dress that was like no other wraparound dress he'd ever seen. This one was held with spaghetti straps that criss-crossed her otherwise bare back. At the front, the shimmering silk plunged in a V to meet at her midriff where bands of the spaghetti straps wrapped around her. When she'd twirled he'd glimpsed the loop low at the base of her spine where the straps tied together, and his blood thickened to imagine untying that knot and spinning her round to unwrap her.

His gaze swept down, following the dress's shimmering path to her feet, which were pretty in a pair of three-inch-heeled gold Roman-style sandals, then raked back up, over the bands around her waist, up the plunging V, where hints of breast were exposed, and finally back to the heavenly face and the thick sweep of fiery hair loose around her shoulders.

'Incredible,' he breathed.

Elsa felt herself glow at the thrill of his reaction to her appearance even as she absorbed every inch of *him*. There was nothing extraordinary about his outfit—not extraordinary for Santi anyway: black Egyptian cotton shirt, tailored black trousers, tailored charcoal waistcoat and handmade brogues. On his wrist was the watch he'd been wearing five years ago, around his neck the chain that had lived there for as long as she could remember him. Which was for ever.

She'd seen him in many different variations of the outfit but it felt like she was seeing him for the first time tonight. All the parts that made the total of him. The black beard and curly black hair. The creases around his eyes. The sparkle *in* his eyes. The muscles straining against his shirt. The rise and fall of his chest.

Her heart was fluttering madly, as if joy and excitement had been let loose together.

He held his elbow out. 'Shall we?'

She stepped forward as gracefully as she could considering her feet were straining to spring themselves at him, and slipped her hand into the crook, and happily let him lead her into the warm Mallorca night.

Elsa peered through the windows of the luxury car that had collected them from the marina. They'd driven through the beautiful village of Cala Deia with its honey-coloured homes, and affluent holidaymakers and residents alike enjoying the evening warmth in local restaurants and bars, and then taken a remote road, ascending through thick woodland until reaching a high iron gate that blocked further travel. An armed security guard approached from the sentry box to the right of the gate. Santi lowered his window and plucked a business card from his wallet, which he showed to the unsmiling guard who studied it before tapping something into a phone.

The iron gates slowly opened to reveal immaculately maintained grounds surrounding a sprawling sand-coloured villa.

'What is this place?' she asked as the car crawled to the villa's entrance, thinking it must be a luxury hotel.

'Club Giroud,' Santi said.

'Really?' Elsa hadn't thought her mood could feel any perkier considering she already felt that she was floating on air, but it did. She'd tried to sneak into the über-exclusive members-only club's Madrid venue once with a school friend who'd stolen her mother's membership card but both girls had been refused entry. Her surname had been no match for the stern doormen.

Santi picked up on her excitement and laughed. 'Really.'

'How long have you been a member?'

'A few years. It's good for networking.'

No sooner had they stopped than the two men standing guard at the bottom of the steps of the entrance opened their doors.

They climbed the steps with their hands clasped together.

'I hope you're not planning to network tonight,' she murmured.

'With you on my arm?' he said, feigning horror. 'I'd be too worried about someone whisking you away from me.'

'You should definitely keep me close to your side. To stop that happening,' she added.

'Don't worry.' They swept through the huge double doors that parted for them like the Red Sea. 'I'm not letting you out of my sight.'

Not for a second.

A hostess greeted them like old friends in the vast reception room and then they were led up two flights of cantilevered stairs. They continued down a long corridor where music and laughter could be heard coming from the myriad rooms they passed, then up another flight of stairs until they were on the roof terrace. Elsa couldn't help but sigh her pleasure at the sight that greeted her.

She hadn't realised how high up the villa was located and from this spot and this vantage point it seemed the whole of the western Mallorca coastline was spread out before her. The yachts in the distant anchorage bay seemed like toy boats bobbing amongst the waves. With the stars out in force on this moonless night, the whole setting was enough to make the heart sing.

Santi heard Elsa's dreamy sigh and smiled. Of all the Clubs Giroud scattered around the world, this, the most recently developed of them, was a significant departure from its usual gothic-inspired luxury. Possibly the setting had inspired the change to something more romantic.

Mallorca was a holiday destination. Club Giroud members who came here to dine would likely have partners and families in tow. The terrace was proof of this theory, as couples and families alike dined in the open air. He spotted Luis Casillas, a fellow club member he'd got to know in recent years and whose company he enjoyed, dining with his beautiful wife Chloe and their small daughter, and waved a hand in greeting as they passed.

They were shown to a table by the sandstone balustrade.

'Can I get you drinks?' their hostess asked when they were seated.

Elsa hesitated for only a moment before saying, 'A white wine spritzer for me.'

Santi raised a brow but held off saying anything until the hostess had gone.

A dress that showed three times as much flesh as anything else he'd seen her in and now this? 'Alcohol, *chiquita*?'

She gave a smile of such contentment that it pierced straight through his heart. 'It's time, don't you think?'

'What I think is irrelevant.'

'Not to me,' she contradicted softly. 'But what you said, about me needing to let the past go…it resonated. I *like* wine, and I'm old enough to know when to stop.' Then her mouth made the swirling motion and she added with a cackle, 'I don't think I can ever look a measure of rum in the eye again, though.'

Laughing, he took her hand and tugged it to his mouth so he could graze the knuckles with kisses.

Soon they were eating their way through courses of divinely cooked food and stealing forkfuls of each other's dishes and exchanging stories of the five years they'd missed from each other's lives. It was incredible to think that this beautiful woman, laughing throatily as she taught him how to swear fluently in German, was the same closed-off, frightened woman he'd met up with in Vienna a few days ago.

He'd just finished his lobster when Luis Casillas, carrying his sleepy daughter, waved goodbye and made a 'call me' sign.

Santi stuck his hand in the air in acknowledgement, and found his gaze following the Casillas family as they left the terrace with the strangest pang rippling in his chest at the closeness they so obviously shared.

He drained his wine. He wasn't there to mourn what could have been. He was there to enjoy his final night with the most beautiful woman to inhabit the earth.

He indicated Elsa's empty plate. 'Dessert?'

'Try and stop me.'

He grinned. 'What would you like to do after?'

'What are the options?'

'Off the top of my head, the club has a casino, a nightclub, a jazz room—don't pull faces, *chiquita*, some people like jazz—and a—'

'The nightclub,' she interrupted decisively.

'You want to dance?'

Her eyes flashed. 'I want to dance with *you*.'

CHAPTER TWELVE

THE NIGHTCLUB WAS busier than Elsa had anticipated and had a far more glamorously seductive vibe than she'd expected too. So wrapped up in her Santi cloud had she been that it was a shock to bump into her old schoolfriend Lola. The porcelain heiress couldn't wait to show Elsa the ridiculously ostentatious diamond engagement ring flashing on her finger before introducing her to the man who'd bought it, an Italian aristocrat who liked to be accorded his defunct title of Conte.

When Lola took a breath from gushing about her wedding plans and clocked Santi, chatting to her fiancé and club members he was acquainted with, her eyes widened and she snatched Elsa's hand to drag her to the ladies.

'You and Santi?' she squealed. 'I can't believe you've finally pulled him. How long's it been going on? Tell me everything! I'm so jealous!'

'What are you jealous for?' Elsa asked drily, neatly sidestepping the other rapid-fire questions. 'You've got yourself a *conte*.'

Lola's eyes sparkled as much as her engagement ring.

'I know. But you have to admit... Santi...' She fanned her face with her hand. 'He's so *masculine*! Remember when we all fancied him? What's he like in bed? I bet he's *amazing*...'

'Have you set a date for the wedding?' Elsa interrupted with a smile. Five years ago she would probably have thrilled in sharing every little detail with her friend, but now... What she shared with Santi was private. Special. Wonderful.

Lola took the bait and happily blathered on about her extravagant plans while they made their way back to their partners.

Santi had moved to a round table on the edge of a dance floor and was clearly keeping watch for her as his eyes locked onto hers as soon as she re-entered the room. The crowd around him had grown in her short absence and he was chatting to a tall man she recognised. She smiled a greeting, sure he was the brother of another old schoolfriend, but before she could say hello she found herself pulled into an embrace by another face from the past.

Santi watched Elsa laugh as she disentangled herself from yet another pair of arms. Was there anyone she didn't know? All these faces, men and women of the kind he'd carefully cultivated working relationships with, these were Elsa's peers. Spain's elite. If he took her to any Club Giroud in Europe, she was bound to bump into someone she knew.

A crowd gathered around her, wanting to hear about her life in Vienna. Where it had taken Santi a good few years and a few extra billion in the bank to feel accepted in places like this, Elsa simply sidled in and was embraced by everyone. This was her world. She'd stepped out of it for five years but was welcomed back as if no time had passed.

Santi was accepted but he didn't belong, not in the way Elsa did. He was the interloper, the mimic octopus able to change colour and pass itself off as different sea creatures. He was a bad-mannered kid from the poorest part of Seville. All the trappings he'd accumulated over the past decade didn't change that. He didn't belong.

His beautiful Elsa did, and one day she would marry a man worthy of her, maybe one of the men making subtle eyes at her now. A man born and raised in her world.

But she was still his for one more night and with a determination to make every minute count, he extracted himself from his conversation and weaved over to her.

Her smile as their eyes met dazzled him.

By the time they left the club, Elsa was no longer floating on air but soaring giddily over the clouds.

Who needed alcohol to feel drunk when dancing with Santi induced that same intoxicated feeling? Just being with him did.

She snuggled up to him in the back of the car, head on his chest, and closed her eyes to remember it all. The darkly illuminated, sensual nightclub. The pulsing dance music that had vibrated through her feet. The jostling of other dancers around them forcing her to attach herself like a barnacle to Santi...or so she'd told him, she remembered with a stifled giggle. Her surprise when Santi had thrown some moves that had had her clapping with delight. The time she'd used the ladies and had found him waiting outside for her and then pressing her against the wall for a kiss so deep and passionate that she'd been throbbing all over when he'd pulled away with a seductive grin.

It had been the best night of her life.

'Drink?' Santi offered when, hands clasped, they stepped back onto the yacht.

Her mesmerising eyes sparkled. 'Anything but rum.'

He rummaged in the small bar and found an unopened bottle of bourbon. He dropped ice in Elsa's glass then poured them both a measure before passing hers.

She accepted it with a sensual smile and raised the glass for him to chink.

Eyes fixed on her face, he took a slow sip. She copied him, barely flinching when the alcohol hit her throat, then, deliberately, poked her pink tongue out and ran it over her top lip.

The arousal that had risen and ebbed but had always been there throughout the night stirred.

What a night it had been. Relief that the nightmare of the cartel was over mingled with the lust and delight they'd found in each other had made it a fitting finale to an incredible week.

And it wasn't over. Not quite yet.

He took a step towards her.

Eyes gleaming, she took a step back.

He took another step forward.

She took another step back…then beckoned with her finger and turned to bound down the steps to her cabin.

Like a disciple tailing his leader, he followed in her wake.

The blinds of the cabin had already been drawn. Illumination from the marina filtered through them and blended with the light streaming in through the open door to cast the cabin in shades of grey.

She stood at the far end of the bed. Their eyes locked. She swallowed the last of her drink and placed her empty glass on the small dining table. She stepped over to him. And then she turned her back.

He gently fingered the knot of her straps at the base of her spine before doing what he'd fantasied about doing all those hours ago. He tugged at the knot. It loosened a little. He tugged again. It came undone. And then the dress fell apart.

He sucked in a breath.

He'd spent the evening lusting over this woman, having not the faintest idea that beneath the beautiful dress she was naked.

His throat closed, stifling the groan about to escape. His loins were on fire. *He* was on fire.

One quick shrug and the dress fell to her feet like a sheet. Still wearing her heels, she stepped over it and placed a hand to his chest. 'Your turn,' she whispered.

First she unbuttoned his waistcoat. Then she unbuttoned his shirt. Once that was removed and added to the growing pile on the floor, her hands went to his trousers.

Eyes still holding his, she fumbled for a moment before she managed to undo the belt. There was no fumbling with the button or zipper.

She stripped him naked without laying a finger on an inch of his burning flesh.

Done, she took a step back and appraised him like a lion about to strike its prey.

Santi had never been more turned on in his life.

'On the bed,' she ordered huskily.

He could hardly move his legs to obey. They felt as drugged as the rest of him.

Elsa watched this beautiful man whom she loved more than anything in the world lay himself in the middle of the bed. Her heart was so full she could barely breathe.

Her love for him had sneaked up on her during their wonderful evening together. It had started when she'd felt so protective about what they'd found together under Lola's deluge of questions, and had crystallised when a flare of panic had ripped her chest after losing sight of him for twenty seconds.

Her heart had given itself back to him. To fight it or deny it any longer was to live in more delusion.

Santi was her anchor. The one person she could always depend on. When she'd woken that morning, terrified of what the day would bring, her chest feeling like it had been injected with liquid nitrogen, she'd automatically rolled into his arms for warmth and comfort. For safety.

She was emotionally ready for him now, which she

hadn't been before. Her years in Vienna had taught her independence and resilience—even if she hadn't learned how to cook, she thought with a giggle that cut through her stupor—and given her the tools to hold her own with him.

Her teenage love had been more of an obsession. An infatuation.

This felt solid. Deep. Abiding.

She'd fantasised all night about doing this. About making love to *him*.

No shame. No shyness. No self-loathing. Just this. Just them.

He'd done this to her. Santi had helped her to fix herself. He'd chased the shadows away. He'd helped her become the woman she'd always wanted to be.

Moving steadily to him, she kicked her sandals off then parted his legs and crawled onto the bed between them. Hands at his ankles, she dragged them slowly up over his muscular calves and even more muscular thighs. The only sound from Santi was the raggedness of his breathing.

His eyes stayed wide open, fixed on her. The thrill she felt to see the look in them had her closing her own and breathing deeply to keep control of herself. She ached to have him inside her, for their bodies to be crushed together, but there was something she needed to do first.

She straddled him as she'd done earlier on the sundeck, when she'd had to be clothed to do it. She'd teased him. Tormented him. Revelled in the power she had over him in this wonderful way.

Her old demons no longer had power over her.

She stretched forward. The tips of her breasts brushed against his chest. She extended an arm and found the bedside light switch, and turned it on.

Santi lay there, fire burning through his veins, and was suddenly certain he'd died and gone to heaven. Elsa had turned the light on and then had sat back up, her sex gently rubbing against the tip of his erection.

For once, the relief he would have found thrusting straight into her was not the first thing on his mind. He was too entranced at seeing her display her beautiful body for him without an ounce of shyness. He wouldn't have been able to stop his greedy eyes from devouring every inch of her perfection if he had wanted to.

She traced her fingers over his hand then lifted it and placed it over a perfectly plump, high breast and exhaled a sigh. Her erect nipple rubbed against his palm.

He ran his fingers over the other breast. Felt her shiver.

Resting her hands lightly on his chest, she slowly sank down on him. He dragged a hand from her perfect breast to grip her hip, holding her steady.

And then he waited, too intoxicated with what was happening to draw air in.

Eyes fixed on his, she moved slowly, rising up to the tip and then sinking back down.

It was the most erotic thrill of Santi's life.

She rode him slowly, then gradually increased the

tempo. He couldn't tear his eyes from her face, soaking in the way desire heightened the colour of her cheeks, the way her lips parted and soft moans fell, the way her eyes fluttered closed, the way her head swayed...

Elsa fought to hold on and savour this heady moment just a little longer but it was a fight she couldn't win, not with the glorious sensations building so deeply inside her, and when she felt her orgasm swell and break free, she threw her head back and cried his name as she rode the peak. The waves of pleasure ravaging her deepened when he suddenly sat up and covered her breast with his mouth before kissing her lips and wrapping his arms around her. Still riding the waves, Elsa threw her arms around him, holding tightly as he bucked furiously into her, his own release coming with a roar that echoed right through to her bones and into her frantically beating heart.

Santi turned the light off and enveloped Elsa in his arms. She wriggled a thigh between his legs and kissed his chest. His body craved sleep but his brain was still wired, reliving every minute of what they had just shared. Sensation still buzzed through him.

For a man who'd always rolled over and fallen unconscious straight after sex, the nights spent holding Elsa were like nothing he'd ever experienced. He would miss the closeness and affection as much as he missed her.

He ran his fingers gently up and down her spine. She made a noise much like a purring cat.

Slowly, the buzz in his veins settled, his thoughts dispersed and sleep pulled him into its clutches.

'Do you think it'll feel different between us when we get back home?'

His eyes snapped open.

Elsa's chin was on his chest. He could feel her staring at him.

He blinked vigorously, trying to clear his mind from the fog of sleep.

Her fingers tiptoed up his throat and rubbed against the bristles of his beard. 'This whole trip has been like a rollercoaster,' she said dreamily. 'It's strange as it's been one of the worst times of my life but it's been one of the best too. *The* best. I can't wait to see my family but I'm going to really miss this. Can we get away again soon, just the two of us? Take to the road or seas and just follow our noses?'

Elsa babbled on with a slowly tightening chest.

Why wasn't he responding? She knew by his breathing that he was awake.

'I keep imagining us going about our normal lives without all this drama and adrenaline, and—'

His hand suddenly gripped hold of hers. 'Elsa, stop.'

An icy prickle of dread pierced her heart. She lifted her head. 'What's wrong?'

His chest rose sharply before he released her hand and pulled away from her, straightening as he swung his legs off the bed.

His abrupt withdrawal left her chilled inside and

out, and she fumbled for the bedside light, needing to look at his face and search it for what could be wrong.

When the dim light saturated the room, he hunched over and kneaded the back of his head.

She put a tentative hand to his shoulder. The muscles tensed at her touch. The prickle of dread was fast threatening to run into panic. 'What's wrong?' she repeated.

His words when they came were hoarse. 'When we get home, there is no us. I thought you knew that.'

A punch in the throat would have shocked her less, and had exactly the same effect. For the longest time she couldn't move it to speak. After numerous futile attempts, all she managed was, 'Santi?'

He twisted round to face her and covered the nape of her neck with his hand, gently holding her still while he stared into her eyes. 'This thing between us...' A grimace of pain flittered over his face. 'It can't go anywhere.'

Her bewilderment was stark and cut Santi to the quick.

'I don't understand,' she said in a strangely childlike voice.

He pressed his forehead to hers. 'It can never work between us.'

'But...but... Why? How can you know that?'

'I've always known it. I thought you did too.' Hadn't he made it clear? Hadn't it been as obvious to her as it had been to him?

Now cradling her head, he stared intently into her bewildered eyes. 'We've shared a unique experience.

You said it yourself; a rollercoaster. We've been running on adrenaline and heightened emotions. Whatever attraction it set off…if it hadn't been for the circumstances, none of it would have taken root. When we're home things will feel very different, and you know it too—you just said it yourself. Sure, we could try and carry it on but it wouldn't last because it wouldn't be the same. It wouldn't feel the same.'

'You don't know that.'

'I do.'

A tear rolled down her cheek. 'You're not even prepared to try?'

He was going to hurt her. He *was* hurting her.

God forgive him. This was the last thing he'd wanted to do.

He'd eat glass for this woman. He'd take a dozen bullets for her and then come back for more.

He forced his voice to be steady so she wouldn't hear the lie, and hardened his heart. 'No. I'm not.'

This wasn't a mere punch in the throat. This landed like a full-on body-blow, and Elsa only managed to stop herself doubling over by summoning every ounce of pride she possessed.

He must have read something of her feelings for he took her trembling hand and pressed a kiss to it but the blunt justifications for breaking her heart continued. 'I have had the *best* time with you but we've been in a bubble. As soon as we land in Valencia, the bubble will burst. *Chiquita*, you're going to make some lucky man very happy but that someone can't be me. You deserve better.'

She snatched her hand away and shuffled back, trying desperately to retain some kind of dignity as she wrapped the sheets tightly around herself. A piercing of agony shot through her to know she'd opened herself to him, heart, body and soul. She'd given him the last of herself only that night because she'd believed...

'These days...' She cleared her throat. Nausea churned in her stomach, growing in intensity as the implications of what Santi was saying became clearer. All the hopes and dreams she'd allowed back into daylight...

One giant delusion when the lesson she'd learned at Santi's hands five years ago was not to indulge in delusion.

'These days we've spent as lovers,' she managed to continue, fighting with all her might not to let her anguish seep into her voice. 'You knew all along that once we left this yacht then that would be it for us?'

His face tightened into a grimace. 'At no point did we discuss a future together. Not once. You spoke of returning to Vienna only yesterday.'

'Yes, but...'

But that was before I realised I was in love with you, when I was still in denial, and even then I never thought we would be over the minute we disembarked. I never realised you saw me as only a quick fling.

'I said only a few hours ago that we needed to make

the most of our last night together,' he said in the same clipped tone. 'How could you misinterpret that?'

'I thought you meant our last night together *here*. Like this. Before real life reclaimed us.'

'I'm sorry you misunderstood.'

'I'm good at that, aren't I?' An acrid taste filled her mouth. 'But what did *you* think, Santi? That we'd skip off this yacht together and exchange one last tender kiss before, by telepathic mutual agreement, going our separate ways?'

His jaw clenched so tightly the bones threatened to poke out. His silence confirmed her fears. And roused her anger.

'Did you seriously think I would be happy with that?' She couldn't keep the bitterness from vibrating in her voice or her rising pitch. 'Did you see me in the future, gazing out of a window with a dreamy smile on my face as I remembered those wonderful days, just you and me, making love under the sun? Because let me put you right—all I'm going to remember is *this*.'

The moment he broke the heart she'd fought with all her might from giving back to him after he'd shattered it the first time.

No longer looking at her, he got to his feet. 'I'm sorry.'

His muscular legs disappeared into his trousers before he bent over to gather the rest of the clothes she'd stripped from him just a short time ago when she'd so briefly believed they had the foundations of something wonderful. It hurt to look. It hurt to breathe. It hurt to even speak.

But something nagged at her, tapping at her shell-shocked brain.

He closed the adjoining door behind him. For a long time she did nothing but stare at it.

How could Santi make love to her the way he had if all he'd thought of her as was some kind of short holiday fling? The way he'd looked at her. The way he'd touched her...

The nagging voice suddenly became clear.

She scrambled off the bed, grabbed an oversized T-shirt from a drawer and quickly shrugged her arms into it before barging her way into Santi's cabin.

CHAPTER THIRTEEN

'WHAT DID YOU mean about me deserving better?' she demanded.

Santi, who was sitting on the edge of the bed, lifted his head with a sinking heart. He'd known it couldn't end so easily.

'It was a figure of speech,' he lied with a heavy sigh. Everything felt heavy in him right down to the chain he wore around his neck, the last gift from his mother before her death.

Her eyes narrowed. 'Does this have something to do with my parents and what you think you owe them?'

'I don't think, I *know*.'

'You said something the other day about never betraying them. Is that what you see us as? A betrayal?'

He gritted his teeth. He could feel anger stirring in the combustible mix of emotions he was doing his damned best to keep a lid on. Where the anger was coming from he didn't know, but it was in him.

She folded her arms tightly across her chest. Bitterness ravaged her beautiful face. 'That's it, isn't it? It's nothing to do with us being in a bubble.' She stormed over to his unresponsive form and leaned forward to eyeball him with green-brown eyes wild with hurt and anger. 'Deny that you think you and I being together is a betrayal of them.'

Santi concentrated on breathing in and out through his nose, not prepared to open his mouth even for air, fearing that the rancid anger burning through him with all the other tumultuous emotions would burst free.

'Deny it!' she shouted, stabbing a finger into his chest. 'Look me in the eye and deny that you're throwing me away out of stupid, misplaced loyalty.'

He grabbed hold of her wrist before he even knew his hand had moved. '*Misplaced*?' he snarled in her face. 'Your *mamá* trusted me to bring you home to her. She trusted you would be safe with me, just as she and your *papá* trusted me all those years ago to keep you safe and out of the hands of men like me.'

'Men like *you*?'

'I put my teacher in hospital!' he roared. 'I battered him beyond recognition. I should have gone to prison for what I did to that man, so don't you dare accuse me of misplaced loyalty when *you*…' He drew the word out and let it hang.

At that moment he hated her, everything about her, but especially the way she could push his buttons and provoke him to anger and all the other emotions she elicited in him that no one else could.

'You have been pampered and cosseted and spoilt rotten your entire life, and what do you do the first time something doesn't go your way? You run. You ran away like a coward to Vienna because mean old Santi kicked you out of his bed. Where was your loyalty to your family then? To the business you'd promised to join? Your sister lost her partner when she was pregnant but even that wasn't enough to get selfish little Elsa back home where she belonged, not even after your father was killed, so don't you dare speak as if loyalty is something to be scorned when you don't know the meaning of the word.

'The only reason I wasn't locked up is because of your father. Do you think for a minute he or your *mamá* would have done any of the things they did for me if they thought I would take advantage of their precious little Elsa? I have told you countless times that everything I have, I owe to them. Without them, I'd still be that poor, ill-mannered thug. I *am* still him, and knowing I've abused their trust *kills* me. I don't belong in your world and I never have. You think your father isn't turning in his grave at what I've done?'

Her face had turned ashen. Her eyes were wide, staring at him as if he were a stranger. A monster.

But there was no time for guilt to find its way into him for Elsa suddenly yanked her wrist out of his hold and rubbed it as if trying to rid herself of poison.

'The only thing he'll be turning in his grave at is what you're doing to me now,' she said icily. *'He knew.'*

Elsa watched the confusion play out on Santi's expressive face without an ounce of pleasure. She was too busy trying to keep herself upright.

It was his expressive face, she suddenly realised,

that had been the cause of the nagging in her brain. His mouth had been telling her they were over but his eyes had said something very different.

She no longer cared. Santi had just vented his real feelings to her in the clearest and crispest manner. She couldn't misinterpret anything here. Any translator would come to the same conclusion—Santi *did* think she was a spoilt bitch. Something told her his words were going to haunt her for a long time to come but she wouldn't dissect them now, not in front of him, not when her heart felt like it was bleeding into her chest and one wrong word or thought could push her over the edge into a black pit of despair.

But she wouldn't run away. She wouldn't be a coward again. She wouldn't give him the satisfaction.

'Papá sat me down for a private chat when I was sixteen,' she informed him, enunciating every syllable of every word very clearly. 'He told me I was too young for you and that I should try not to make my feelings so obvious in case it made you uncomfortable and that all I had to do was wait a few more years.'

The shock that pulsed in his black eyes would have been funny if hate hadn't settled in her heart. She welcomed the hate and laughed anyway. Even to her own ears it sounded like a witch's cackle but she didn't care. Anything had to be better than the excruciating pain that had come close to paralysing her.

'He knew I was in love with you. He also knew some of what happened that night.'

His jaw dropped. His head shook sluggishly, left to right, right to left.

'He found me crying in my bedroom the night before I left for Vienna. All I told him was that I'd declared my feelings for you and that you'd turned me down—I was far too ashamed to tell him the rest of it. He said I had to be brave, and that life was long and people's feelings change. He said you and I had such a unique bond that all I had to do was hold tight and wait a little longer for you to see me as a woman.' She laughed again. 'Of course, I ignored his advice. After all, he didn't know the disgrace I'd made of myself.'

She forced her eyes to stay locked on Santi's. She would not flinch away from painful truths and memories. Not any more.

She'd never known him be so still. The man who zinged with energy was sitting on the edge of the bed like a statue. Only his eyes, fixed on her, moved.

'The only thing you owed him was to make something good of your life, and you've done that. You've earned your place in this world. Papá loved you like a son. Nothing, and I mean *nothing*, would have made him happier than for you to marry into the family just so he could have the pleasure of calling you that.' A sudden burst of nausea rose up her throat but she swallowed it back and forced herself to continue. 'And now I'm glad—*glad*,' she repeated venomously, 'that I ignored his advice. You're not fit to be called his son.'

He flinched. Good.

'You've strung me along for days. All this time you

knew we had no future together and it's nothing to do with not wanting to abuse my parents' trust, it's because you're a bastard. How you have the nerve to say I need to let go of the past when you wear your past like a shield is beyond me but, still, I'm glad you've told me what you really think of me. Saves me wasting any more tears over you.' She folded her arms over her chest again and forced the muscles on her cheeks to form a smile before she fired her parting shot. 'As far as I'm concerned, you can go to hell.'

And then she stalked out of the cabin, slamming the adjoining door behind her.

Santi gave a sharp rap on the locked adjoining door. 'We need to go.'

There was no answer. He didn't expect one.

Elsa appeared on the deck two minutes after him, suitcase in hand, standing proud and elegant in a pretty cream fitted summer dress, long red hair flowing beneath her wide-brimmed sunhat. Her eyes were hidden behind her shades but he had no sense of her looking at him.

He attempted to take the suitcase from her but she stepped sharply out of his way and pulled it over the gangplank herself. She didn't bother to wait for him, setting off with her head held high.

The silent treatment continued in the back of the car as they were driven to the airport and through the private security clearance. The first words she uttered were a pleasant, 'Thank you,' to his cabin crew when they showed her to her seat on his plane.

When, just after they'd taken off, his next attempt at conversation was rebuffed, he gritted his teeth and opened his laptop. If that's the way she wanted to play it, then fine. He had nothing to say to her anyway. He was just being polite.

He'd barely given his business a thought in the past week. The last time he'd checked in had been at his lodge by the lake in Austria. He couldn't believe how long ago that now felt.

Maybe if he'd given more thought to work during their trip and less to pleasure, he wouldn't have got into this mess, he thought grimly. Sleeping with Elsa had been a mistake, the consequences a mess of his own making.

Part of him wanted to apologise for the cruel things he'd said to her. The other part thought she could damn well join him in the hell she'd told him to go to. The biggest part of him thought he shouldn't think of her at all. So he didn't.

Mercifully, the flight to Valencia was short and he made a little headway with his work, deleting the three hundred and twenty-four emails he'd received since last logging on, before they landed on his private airfield.

He noted, with a sour taste in his mouth, that she was perfectly happy to let one of the cabin crew carry her suitcase off the plane.

Elsa couldn't help being impressed with the set-up at the airfield. This was the European hub of Santi's business. All around her stood ridiculously high warehouses the size of football fields and stacks of cargo containers. As she walked towards the waiting limousine, she took in every detail she could, right down to the scores of workers bustling around them. Anything rather than pay the slightest bit of attention to the man walking silently behind her.

She couldn't even look at him. She didn't dare. But she knew exactly where he was, about three steps behind and slightly to her right. Close but the furthest he'd ever been from her. Or was she the furthest she'd ever been from him?

Last night, after she'd locked the adjoining door, she'd surprised herself by falling asleep almost the moment her head had hit the pillow. She'd surprised herself even more when she'd woken that morning and found that she felt fine. It helped that she had something to focus on, namely returning to her family, and she increased the length of her strides to the limousine. She would be with her *mamá*, her sister and her nephew very soon. As long as she didn't look at Santi or engage in conversation with him, she was certain she would continue to feel fine. Empty inside but fine. No pain.

The driver got out of the limousine and tipped his hat in greeting.

She slid into the back. The driver shut the door. So intent was Elsa in not allowing any part of Santi into her vision that she didn't register the driver getting behind the wheel or putting the car into gear, didn't register anything until the car rolled forward and she realised they were leaving without him.

The panic injected itself straight into her heart without the slightest hint of warning.

'What are you doing?' she yelped into the microphone. 'Santi's not here.'

'Mr Rodriguez has made alternative arrangements,' the driver informed her.

Frantic, she pressed her face against the window, searching desperately for him, but all she could see was the back of his curly hair as he chatted with three of his staff.

He didn't look back.

He didn't see her drive away.

He didn't see the tears fall down her face or hear her muffled howl as the pain she'd boxed in punched its way free and doubled her over.

It took only ten days of living with her mother for Elsa to know she needed to leave. The last time she'd lived under the same roof as her mother she'd been a teenager. She'd made plenty of visits home over the years, often for weeks at a time, but those had always had an end date.

This was different. Elsa had moved back home. She'd resigned from her boring office job—now she really thought about it, she couldn't believe she'd kidded herself that she'd enjoyed it; she'd been bored out of her mind—and had all her possessions couriered over. In ten short days, she and her *mamá* had driven each other crazy. But in a good way. In the comfortable, familiar way they'd driven each other crazy when Elsa had been a teenager but without the added hormonal angst. She needed to leave, but was in no hurry to actually facilitate it. The terror she'd felt on The Trip, as she'd come to call it in her mind, that she could lose her family, was still there in diluted form. She suspected it would be in her for a long time to come.

If she could implant trackers in her mother and sister, she would. And they'd do the same for her. One day soon she would get a place of her own but it would be within a kilometre of them.

She was sitting in the orangery, reading through a pile of paperwork Marisa had given her to read on the family business human resources division, which Elsa was going to take over the running of when the current director retired in three months, when her sister walked in, holding baby Nikos in one arm and a collection of bulging bags hanging off the crook of the other.

'How was it?' Elsa asked. 'Did you find what you wanted?'

Marisa had been shopping for a dress for her engagement party and, despite babysitting offers from Elsa and their *mamá*, had taken baby Nikos with her. Elsa was proud of her—it was the first time Marisa had taken her son anywhere outside the estate. She'd lost her lover and her father within six months of each other. Her baby had been born without a father or a grandfather. Only now, with the cartel's destruction, could she breathe easily enough to take her son out of the estate and into the big wide world.

Elsa struggled with horrendous guilt. Her sister had been through hell and what had she been doing? Hiding and pining. She'd been monstrously selfish, and it didn't matter that Marisa had virtually ordered her back to Vienna after their father's funeral and the birth of her son. Elsa should have stayed. She should have been there for her in person and not just at the end of a phone.

She would make up for it, she vowed. She would be there for her family always and at all times, whether they liked it or not.

Marisa pulled a face. 'I don't know. I couldn't decide which one I liked the most so I bought them all. Will you have a look?'

'Sure.'

In Marisa's bedroom, Elsa settled on the bed with baby Nikos on her lap and waited patiently while her sister put the outfits on and paraded herself for Elsa's opinion.

When she emerged from her dressing room wearing the fifth outfit, a garish creation that made her beautiful sister look like an aubergine, baby Nikos threw his dummy at her.

Marisa burst into laughter and scooped him from Elsa's arms and held him up in the air above her head.

'You clever boy! Your aim is amazing! Your daddy would be proud. And you're right—it's a *horrible* dress. Mamá will take this one back.' Then she looked at Elsa and grinned. 'On second thoughts, maybe I should wear it. Raul will hate it.'

Elsa tried not to wince. With all the drama of the cartel's takedown, Marisa had reluctantly agreed to a short postponement, the engagement party now occurring in two days. Her enthusiasm for her future husband—which had always been tepid at best—had become downright cool in recent days.

She shuffled back to rest against the headboard and patted the space on the bed beside her. 'Come and sit with me.'

Marisa did better than that. Still wearing the horrible dress, she curled onto the bed, put baby Nikos on his back in the curve of her stomach, and laid her head on Elsa's lap, giving Elsa free reign on her corkscrews. Where Elsa's red hair was straight, Marisa's was the opposite, a mass of tight red curls that Elsa had loved playing with since they were tiny.

'Are you sure you want to go ahead with this?' she asked gently.

To give Marisa credit, she didn't pretend not to understand. 'I don't know any more. You joining the business changes things a little but I still need help and Nikos still needs a father.'

'Does it have to be Raul?'

'If not him, then who? Anyone else would want too much from me.'

Elsa understood. Marisa had been deeply in love with baby Nikos's father. She twirled one of the curls in her fingers. 'I don't trust him.'

'Raul?'

'Yes. What protection did he offer when all this with the cartel was going down? Where was he? And where's he been since?'

Nowhere was the answer. Marisa's slime-ball of a fiancé's concern had extended to him dropping over for a quick coffee three days after the cartel had been taken down and taking her out for a meal. This was the man she intended to entrust her life and her son's life to.

Although Elsa took great pains not to think about the man she'd gone on The Trip with, she couldn't help comparing his actions to the slime-ball's. Not forgetting all the stuff he'd done before and during The Trip for her family, he'd since spent a morning on the estate going through their current security arrangements with their security team—luckily, she'd had prior warning and had been able to make herself scarce—and had had three brand-new cars delivered for each of the three Lopez women that would rival tanks for safety.

'I don't know what to do for the best,' Marisa whispered. 'It all seemed so simple before.'

Elsa picked up another curl. 'Go ahead with the engagement party if you must but don't rush into marrying him. If it doesn't feel right then don't do it, and it's not like baby Nikos doesn't have a male influence.'

That influence being Santi. Since being back home, she'd learned he'd taken to dropping in frequently armed with gifts for him, including the humungous fort-like climbing frame in the garden with a slide and swings and monkey bars he'd built himself. With any luck, baby Nikos would be big enough to use it sometime in the next decade.

'Why didn't you ask Santi to marry you?' The question was out before Elsa could stop it.

Marisa twisted a little so her face looked up at Elsa's. She reached up to gently pat Elsa's cheek. 'Because he belongs to you.'

CHAPTER FOURTEEN

SANTI PARKED IN a shaded area to the left of the Lopez villa and slowly crunched his way to the door. When, he wondered, would he approach this villa without apprehension knotting his guts?

Rosaria opened the door with a scowl that looked so much like the scowl her younger daughter gave when she was displeased that his heart came to a shuddering halt. Hands on hips, she scolded, 'Since when do you knock?'

He held his hands up and grinned. 'I'm sorry. I wasn't thinking.' Too apprehensive about the possibility of seeing Elsa.

'Apology accepted but don't do it again. This is your home, now come here and give me a kiss.'

After profuse kisses to the cheeks and a tight embrace was exchanged, Santi followed her inside.

How many times had she told him this was his home? How many times had Marco?

What had stopped him seeing it as such? Was it because he'd never been formally invited to live in it?

Or because the cottage he'd shared with his mother had felt...

The answer suddenly punched him in the face. The *cottage* had been home for him. It was the place he and his mother had been at their happiest. It was filled with the furniture they'd shared, all their memories framed on the walls and surfaces.

The Lopezes hadn't kept him in the cottage because he wasn't good enough or safe enough to live under the same roof as their daughters but because they'd thought he'd want to stay as close to his mother as he could. They'd been thinking of *him*.

Once they'd settled in the living room that overlooked the garden and coffee had been poured, Rosaria's lips made the same swirling movement her daughter's made. 'You look tired.'

'Thank you.' A night out with Luis Casillas in Madrid was to blame for that, although their evening had come to an abrupt end when Luis's wife had called to tell him the youngest of their growing brood had a temperature. Luis had left so quickly it was like he'd channelled his inner roadrunner. Santi had carried on without him, downing shot after shot, trying not to envy his friend's beautiful family and his obvious devotion to them.

He'd woken with a thumping head and a mouth and throat that felt like sandpaper. He'd probably be sleeping it off still if Felipe hadn't called him.

Rosaria laughed. 'So, what brings you here today? You look like there's something you want to tell me.'

How well she read him. As well as his own mother had, and he felt a huge rush of affection for this wonderful woman who'd supported her husband in making the delinquent Santiago Rodriguez feel loved and worth something.

He would not think about the love he'd felt in the arms of her daughter. He couldn't. To remember it and to remember how he'd killed any chance of a future between them was to face the abyss.

He'd thrown it all away.

'Are you okay?'

He blinked. His mind had gone drifting. It kept doing that.

He cleared his throat. 'Felipe called with an update. I told him I'd pass the details to you.'

Before he could go any further, Rosaria rose gracefully from her seat. 'Let me call the girls. They'll want to hear it.'

She strode to the door and bellowed, 'Marisa. Elsa. Santi has news for us.'

Elsa's blood had stopped flowing. Cold white noise whooshed through her ears.

Marisa gave a smile so sad another strip tore off Elsa's heart. 'I'm your sister. Do you think I didn't notice you fall in love with him all those years ago?'

And then their mother's voice called out to them and her heart came to a shuddering halt and her fingers froze in the curl she'd been in the process of pulling apart.

'Marisa. Elsa. Santi has news for us.'

It felt like time had stood still. She might have sat frozen for ever if her sister hadn't gently covered her hand and pulled it away from her hair so she could sit up. 'Take Nikos for me. I need to take this monstrosity of a dress off.'

She obeyed but it was an automatic response. Holding her plump little nephew, who was currently trying to fit his entire fist into his mouth, she tried to get air into her lungs.

Was this what was meant by serendipity?

For ten days she'd gone out of her way to avoid talking about Santi and done her best to block him from her mind. Other than a quick debrief about The Trip, his name hadn't been mentioned by her family in front of her. Not until a few minutes ago.

He belongs to you.

'Are you coming?'

She lifted her head. Marisa had changed back into her jeans and blouse and was staring at her apprehensively.

Elsa passed baby Nikos to her then bit her lip. 'I can't,' she whispered.

Her sister's shoulders lifted before she sat on the edge of the bed and took Elsa's hand in the one not holding the baby. 'Yes, you can. Now dry your eyes. Don't let him see you like this.'

She hadn't felt the tears fall. So many times these past ten days she'd touched her face and been shocked to find it wet. So many times she'd passed a mirror and frightened herself at the redness in her eyes.

So many times she'd seen her *mamá* and her sister exchange looks.

No wonder his name hadn't been mentioned. If this was how she behaved when trying to go about day-to-day life, how would she act if they forced her to talk about him? There probably weren't enough tissues in the whole of Spain to cope.

Her whole 'I'm doing fine' act had been just that. An act.

Another delusion.

But she would get better. With her family swathing her in love, how could she fail to? One day, she would wake and find the crushing pain a little less. She looked forward to that day.

Santi gripped his coffee cup tightly and worked on keeping his expression…expressionless.

He sensed Rosaria watching him closely as they made idle chatter while waiting for her daughters to appear. He suspected she knew that he and Elsa had been lovers.

If Elsa hadn't told him that Marco had not only known about her feelings for him but had approved of them, *welcomed* them, he'd be searching for Rosaria's icy disapproval. It's what he'd have been expecting. Because he was a fool. Too hung up on the mistakes of his past and humble beginnings to accept that everything the Lopez family had done for him had been because they loved him and not out of charitable endeavour. Too hung up on the past to accept he wasn't that rude, delinquent boy any more. He *had* earned his place in this world. He owed the Lopezes nothing but his love.

Elsa had loved him. That was something he accepted completely. In those short, sweet days at sea, she'd given herself to him like no one had ever done before. And he'd given himself to her.

In those short, sweet days he'd fallen totally, madly, irrevocably in love with her. It was a love he'd carried for her for five long years, just waiting for the right moment to spring free into the light.

And he'd thrown it away. He'd taken her love and discarded it like unwanted ocean debris.

He heard footsteps and murmured feminine voices approach the room. God, his hands were trembling. His heart thumped loudly.

Elsa followed Marisa into the room with a pounding heart and on legs that felt injected with water.

Santi rose from his seat and strode to them, placing a smacker of a kiss on baby Nikos's forehead and more refined kisses to Marisa's cheeks. Only politeness, Elsa was sure, made him extend the same courtesy to her, and she squeezed her eyes shut and lifted her chin as she braced herself for impact.

This was always going to happen, she reminded herself. Whatever her personal feelings, Santi was still family. He would always be a part of her life. She had to learn to live with that, especially now she was home for good.

The kiss, when it came, was over before it began, a

quick brush of his beard against her cheek, the fleeting warmth of his breath against her skin and then done. He was already walking back to his seat before she'd opened her eyes, leaving his earthy, musky scent to torment her.

Her hands had gone clammy, and she wiped them on her jeans before sitting on the sofa next to her sister, pressing herself as close to her as she could. Thankfully, baby Nikos threw himself from his *mamá*'s arms to his aunt's, so she was able to stand him on her lap and hide behind him while Santi relayed his news.

Santi cleared his throat and tried to get his brain to unscramble.

Elsa wouldn't even look at him. He didn't blame her.

'Felipe has updated me on recent developments,' he began, then had to clear his throat again. He'd lost all the moisture in his mouth. 'Firstly, the cartel members who escaped have been arrested.'

Rosaria and Marisa both slumped and closed their eyes with relief. Only Elsa, too busy making faces at her nephew, gave no reaction.

'Secondly, the cartel members who came before the judge in New York have been denied bail.' That meant all of them would remain behind bars until their trials began. 'And thirdly...' he laced his fingers tightly, knowing the effect the next piece of information would have '...one of their members has struck a plea bargain. He's confessed to being part of the plot to kill Marco and named the other perpetrators directly involved.'

Silence followed this.

He couldn't stop his eyes turning to Elsa…

She was staring straight at him now. Tears fell silently like a stream down her face.

He hadn't thought there was any part of his heart left to break.

The thought of justice for their beloved father and husband was not something any of the Lopez women could celebrate. Not yet. They were too shell-shocked. None of them had believed the day would come. There had been days when Santi had struggled to believe it too.

He answered their many questions—well, Rosaria's and Marisa's; Elsa remained mute—over another coffee and then got to his feet. 'I need to go now,' he said before kissing Rosaria and Marisa goodbye.

Then he kissed Nikos and fixed his gaze on the still seated Elsa. 'Can I have a private word, please? It won't take long.'

'I'll take Nikos,' Marisa said, pulling him off her sister's lap before Elsa could refuse. 'Come on, Mamá. Let's give them some privacy.'

Elsa was trapped with him before her stunned brain had time to know what was happening. She arranged her face into her best attempt at nonchalance, crossed her legs and lifted her head, striking the pose her *mamá* had used when she'd demanded to know why Elsa's school report was littered with comments like 'Could try harder'.

Santi was on his feet. He rammed his hands in his

pockets as he paced the room. If she didn't know better, she would think he was nervous.

'I owe you an apology,' he said heavily, coming to a stop in front of her.

She gave no reaction. She couldn't. Suddenly, she felt paralysed.

An apology was the last thing she'd expected.

'What I said to you that night in Mallorca...' Santi swallowed. What he had to say should have been said ten days ago. Every day he'd woken to darkness. Every day his first thought had been of Elsa, and the last thought, and every waking thought in between. 'It was unforgivable. I make no excuses. I was wrong to call you selfish. Everything I said was wrong. I lashed out. I think...' He grimaced. 'I think I lashed out the way I did because I wanted you to hate me. The pain I could see I was putting you through—it cut through me. Do you understand?'

She didn't answer. There wasn't a flicker of expression on her face.

'I couldn't bear to see it. Your pain. When you bleed, I bleed. When you hurt, I hurt.'

Still no expression.

'I'd spent so many years telling myself I wasn't good enough for you that I didn't dare imagine a future with you. I thought I had to end things but inside I was fighting it—my *heart* was fighting it. I thought it was wrong to feel the way I do about you but the only thing that was wrong was me.'

Her eyes closed. A solitary tear trickled down her cheek.

A burning sensation he'd not felt since the death of his mother stung behind his eyes. He pinched the bridge of his nose and took some deep breaths in a futile attempt to counter it. 'I'm sorry I hurt you, *chiquita*. If I could take those cruel words back, I would. You are...' He broke away with a muttered curse and impatiently wiped away dampness around his eyes with his thumbs.

'You are the most important person in my life. You have been for a very long time. I didn't know it was possible to love someone as much as I love you or how deeply I would feel it. It's like you're a part of me. The biggest part of me. And I sure as hell didn't know it was possible to miss someone as much as I miss you. Every day without you hurts a little more. What you said about us taking to the road or seas and following our noses... I can't tell you how badly I wish I'd reacted differently to that because, *chiquita*, I would follow you anywhere.'

The slow blink of her eyes told him he'd said too much. It was the only movement she'd made the whole time he'd been talking.

Ramming his hands back into his pockets, he attempted a smile and failed. 'I should go.'

She blinked again.

He left the room and strode to the front door, staring straight ahead so he didn't have to acknowledge the two women and small child hovering close by. Down the steps and across the gravel he pounded, not stopping until the door to his car was open and he was secure inside.

Only then did he put his face in his hands and weep for the first time since his mother had died.

'Elsa?'

She snapped her eyes open to the concerned faces of her *mamá* and her sister.

Marisa crouched in front of her. 'What did he say?'

She shook her head slowly. 'He… He… *Loves* me.'

It had finally penetrated her stupefied brain.

Santi loved her.

It hadn't been a delusion.

He loved her.

She jumped to her feet so quickly she banged into Marisa and sent her sprawling onto her bottom.

'Sorry,' she cried over her shoulder, already halfway out of the living room and racing towards the front door.

The sun shone so brightly that the first touch of it blinded her. Only her absolute determination to get to Santi stopped her from stumbling.

Her heart crashed to a stop. His car was reversing out from its spot beneath the cherry tree and then, with her next breath, was put into gear and accelerating down the driveway.

She screamed his name at the top of her lungs and then, even though she knew it was hopeless, began to run after him.

As she pushed herself faster than she'd ever run before, her mind flew over the unrelenting misery of the past ten days. She'd been like a wounded bird that had lost its song but still tried to sing.

She'd been surrounded by the love of her family but the nights had been the loneliest of her life.

His car had almost disappeared. At any moment he would reach the electric gates. She couldn't reach him in time. In desperation, she waved her arms in the air, screaming his name over and over.

Santi slowed for the electric gates. As they opened with the speed of a snail on Valium, he wiped his eyes again.

The gap in the gates was almost wide enough to get through, just a few more seconds...

What was that?

Something had caught his attention. He looked around him then suddenly saw it in his rear-view mirror. The figure in the middle of the drive waving their arms and...

Without a moment's thought, he stuck the car in reverse.

Elsa could hardly see through the tears. Santi's car was just a black blob in the distance. Her thighs were screaming at her, her voice was gone and there was a stitch forming in her belly. She didn't stop, still ploughing forward, still waving, still...

The shape of the car changed. It became less of a blur, like it was closing on her...

Seconds later, barely two metres in front of her, it screeched to a stop, the driver's door flew open and Santi got out.

She didn't hesitate. She threw herself at him. Literally. She jumped into his arms without any fear that he wouldn't catch her. Her legs wrapped around his waist, her arms around his neck, his arms wrapped around her and their mouths found each other for a kiss of such passionate ferocity that if she'd had any lingering doubt it would have dissolved.

But she had no doubts. None at all.

She pulled her mouth away so she could gaze into the black eyes shining with pure, heartfelt emotion. 'I love you, Santiago Rodriguez. I've always loved you. I would follow you anywhere.'

The look on his face at this was something Elsa would remember for the rest of her life.

It was the moment their stars finally aligned and they both knew they would spend the rest of their lives together.

EPILOGUE

SANTI LIT THE match and held it to the kindling, dropping it when the small flames began to lick. He added some larger kindling and only when he was satisfied it had a good hold did he add the logs. Then he stepped back, placed the high fireguard around it and considered it with satisfaction.

There was something wonderfully primal about making a fire, he decided, and when his wife joined him in the lodge's snug wearing only a white towelling robe, hair damp from her bath, he felt something even more primal take root. Three years of marriage and his desire for her hadn't abated by an inch.

Snow fell heavily outside. Knowing how much Elsa loved to watch it, he'd kept the curtains open. He imagined Marisa and Rosaria, both retired to their rooms upstairs, enjoying the same magical scene.

The mulled wine was keeping warm, and he poured them both a cup, then stretched out beside her on the sofa.

'I'm afraid you'll have to drink this for me,' Elsa

said, handing her cup back to him with a small knowing smile.

For a moment he was disconcerted. His beautiful wife was hardly a heavy drinker but only the other week, when they'd reached the tail end of their third voyage around the Caribbean on their yacht, she'd been happily sharing exotic cocktails with him…providing they had no rum in them, of course.

And then the penny dropped.

After three years of selfish togetherness, they'd finally decided a month ago that they were ready to create a family.

He twisted to look more closely at her face. His beautiful wife was glowing.

'You're not?' he breathed. How could it be possible? He'd never imagined it would happen so quickly.

She beamed. 'I am. Merry Christmas.'

He shook his head. He was going to be a father…?

He was going to be a father!

He made love to his wife in front of the log fire thinking he'd never imagined such happiness could exist.

* * * * *

Enchanted by
The Forbidden Innocent's Bodyguard?
Look out for the next instalment of the
Billion-Dollar Mediterranean Brides miniseries!

Don't forget to check out these other stories
by Michelle Smart, too!

Her Sicilian Baby Revelation
His Greek Wedding Night Debt
A Baby to Bind His Innocent
The Billionaire's Cinderella Contract
The Cost of Claiming His Heir

All available now

#3913 HER IMPOSSIBLE BABY BOMBSHELL
by Dani Collins

After his challenging upbringing, billionaire Jun Li made sure he *couldn't* have children. So when Ivy Lam, the woman he shared one mesmerizing encounter with, claims she's pregnant, he needs proof—before he claims them *both*!

#3914 PREGNANT IN THE KING'S PALACE
Claimed by a King
by Kelly Hunter

The kingdom thought King Valentine's abdication was his biggest scandal... But given the rebellious royal's fiery reunion with headstrong Angelique, could she be carrying an even more shocking secret?

#3915 STOLEN IN HER WEDDING GOWN
The Greeks' Race to the Altar
by Amanda Cinelli

After the news Greek playboy Eros has just shared about her convenient groom, Priya *can't* walk down the aisle of her Manhattan wedding. To save her father's business, she must flee in her white dress...and wed Eros instead!

#3916 ITALIAN'S SCANDALOUS MARRIAGE PLAN
by Louise Fuller

To win back his bride, Ralph must prove to Juliet he never betrayed her. His plan? Whisk her away for an impromptu night aboard his yacht and remind her of the passionate connection that will make or break their marriage...

#3917 FROM EXPOSÉ TO EXPECTING
by Andie Brock

Following one sexy night with Leonardo, journalist Emma is left mortified by his swift rejection. Letting off steam, she writes a private, scandalous exposé on the tycoon...that's accidentally *published*! Yet that's nothing compared to the surprise that follows...

#3918 THE PLAYBOY'S "I DO" DEAL
Signed, Sealed...Seduced
by Tara Pammi

Dev Kohli's superyacht is the perfect hideout from the forced marriage Clare Roberts is escaping—despite the intimacy it brings... But when the threat to her increases, so does the need to protect her with something Dev never thought he'd offer—his ring!

#3919 HIS BILLION-DOLLAR TAKEOVER TEMPTATION
The Infamous Cabrera Brothers
by Emmy Grayson

Everleigh Bradford's lost too much already to simply hand over control of the family vineyard she expected to inherit. If she must confront internationally renowned new owner Adrian Cabrera, she will! *And* fight her red-hot response to the brooding Spaniard...

#3920 QUEEN BY ROYAL APPOINTMENT
Princesses by Royal Decree
by Lucy Monroe

As a naive teenager, Lady Nataliya signed a contract promising her to a prince. Now to release them both, she causes a scandal. It works... Until her betrothed's brother, the irresistibly brooding King Nikolai, insists she honor the marriage agreement—with *him*!

YOU CAN FIND MORE INFORMATION ON UPCOMING HARLEQUIN TITLES, FREE EXCERPTS AND MORE AT HARLEQUIN.COM.

HPCNMRB0521